Navas

By V.L. Salhotra

For all those dreamers and star gazers

The Void

Before there was everything, there was nothing. Before there was matter, protons, and light, nothingness was prevalent.

The nothingness was a black expanse that filled the entire world at that time and there wasn't a ceiling, fence or gate to contain the blackness. It had been where it had been forever.

The black expanse, or Void, had full rein over how large it wanted to grow and could stretch and pull in any which way it desired. The Void was content in this space, ever growing and ever reaching in its infinite wall-less world.

      The Void soon found that it had stretched and pulled as far as it had wanted to and didn't want to expend any more energy pulling out. It settled, with a deep sigh, and rested for an amount of time.

The Void was beginning to enjoy its solitude, awaiting a long, peaceful breadth of time that it wanted to cherish, now that it had become as large as it needed to be.

However, The Void didn't have the chance to rest for too long.

In the time after, be it seconds or millennia, a small pixel of heavy Void was created in its being.

The Void could feel this pinprick of weight and was too large to locate it, but it gave The Void great discomfort. This pixel was heavier than The Void and began to attract more pixels that grew from The Void's own substance.

The first pixel was now dragging in many other pixels, so much so that The Void could feel pain, then agony, the first time in all of the time it had existed. Eventually, the pixel cluster became a black sphere, spinning to attract further pixels, its size increasing rapidly.

The Void couldn't stop the sphere from gaining momentum, as it hurt. The pain The Void felt was like a knife being twisted and twisted over and over in its side. The Void couldn't scream or shout, but the agony rippled through its entire blackness. The pain reached a point where The Void couldn't cope any

longer and, much to The Void's surprise, the black sphere suddenly split into two.
The second sphere was the same density and size as the first sphere but was a hazy white colour.

The Void was no longer black.

The two spheres rotated in opposite directions to each other but moved in the same rhythm. As they rotated, the white sphere began to take a pixel from the black sphere and vice versa. It was an even exchange and, with each beat, each rotation, one pixel was shared, black to white, white to black.

The Void could feel these two spheres dance in its body, a sore wound that it wondered if it would ever heal from. The Void wanted to close the spheres up into its blackness. In its frustration and anger, it ripped through its own expanse, a tremor the two spheres felt in their cores. The beat of the pixel exchange was off by one, and this modification would forever change the landscape The Void had known.

One pixel, lost between the white and black spheres, became pink and hung between the two oscillating spheres.

The rhythm the spheres had mastered was now off, and the pink pixel watched as the spheres grew and shrank, sucking in far too much or too little colour from each other. There was a battle, a tug of which sphere should remain in The Void.

The spheres never regained their calm exchange.

It became too much for either sphere to fight fairly and, in an act of desperation, the two spheres collided with one another.

There was a symphony of colours that resulted from this collision. In that split second, matter formed, creating atoms, particles, solids and gases. Protons, electrons and elements were all birthed quickly, and their forms filled The Void, taking away the dominant black space.

    Gases were meshed to form stars, and rocks collided to form planets. Heat was generated in the once-frigid Void. The Void was shocked at the new energy permeating it, its black now filled with activity and colour – reds, greens and blues, as colourful and sudden as swiftly blooming flowers.

The pink pixel still floated on its own and marvelled at the world around it. For so long, all it had ever known was black. As it watched the matter and gases and rocks form into giant bodies, the pixel saw a cloud of stars slowly spiral into nothingness. The cloud of stars became a galaxy, its long arms trailing off into The Void. At its centre was a brilliant luminosity.

It was then that the pink pixel realised The Void wanted the black back.

It was taking the light away, so that it could return to its cold, sleeping stretch of blackness. The Void didn't realise that, in its attempt to take the radiance of the world away, it had created a serene disc of light and illumination.

As the pixel watched on, a green pixel of light escaped the galaxy forming and darted around the pink pixel itself. As the two pixels danced around each other like little fairies, they accidentally touched and instantly became two, starlit beings, in a bloom of glitter and shimmer.

One being was male and the other was female. They looked like humans made out of lights, but these lights were stars; they had no real form, but a hazy green light glowed over the female and a pink glow over the male. They were hairless, almost featureless, and it was their outlines that betrayed their indeterminate shape. They resembled humans, if humans were made up of stars and galaxies. Only close up could you see the stars around their mouths drift into a smile, or the glitter focus to become eyes.

Floating in the new space, they stared at each other for a long time.

"Where am I?" the female asked, her voice high and unsure.

"You're... we're... home. This is home now," the male replied calmly.

The female looked around at the kinetic show. Having come from such a stationary existence in The Void to here, where nothing stood still, was overwhelming.

"All I knew was the black," she said softly. "There is so much colour here and light. I feel like it's so new and so familiar at the same time."

The male tilted his head and smiled sweetly.

"I agree. I wonder if you have come from the white sphere or the black sphere?"

The female clasped her hands together over her chest.

"I think we are from the same sphere."

The male floated towards her, and she backed off quickly.

"I won't hurt you."

She stayed a distance from him. "Are you from The Void, then? Or are you light?"

The male opened his arms. "I am of the light. The Void... the blackness... is angry. Can you feel it? He is taking the light back."

The male pointed to the galaxy, the disc of light falling to its doom. "There was a battle that took place. The victor created all of this."

The female watched the galaxy quietly. "Then... I want to see everything. Before it goes. I want to treasure this light before The Void takes it all away."

The male nodded and slowly drifted over to the female and faced her. Gently, he took her sparkling hands and said to her sweetly, "You are my companion in this world. I want to see it all with you."

She smiled and looked away bashfully. With her delicate hand firmly in his, they drifted off into the new space, awestruck at the intense sights. The two beings were massive themselves.

Neatly crafted galaxies could fit into the palms of their hands, and stars could be worn as earrings, but there were bigger entities out there compared to them. The two beings were surprised to see towering stars that were the size of mountains and gas clouds that were barely lit but stretched out for miles back into the black Void.

Deeper still they travelled, and they saw galaxies that were the size of oceans, flat discs that held so much light and energy. The galaxies lit the black area around it like beacons of shattered glass. As quickly as stars were being born, they were also being taken away.

The two explored the space as beings in an astral garden, kneeling to see the little planets or craning their necks to see the tops of stars. The male held the female's hand,

and, despite the warmth of the stars, it was her touch that gave him comfort.

They stopped at a blue star, its light and energy hypnotising the female. She reached out and touched the swirling hot fire of the star and, as she pulled her fingertip away, a tuft of soft blue flame was dragged away from the surface. She smiled in fascination.
"It's so warm," she said delightedly. "Why would The Void want to destroy this?" The male hugged her from behind.
"The Void isn't in control anymore. Here."
She turned to see he was holding a galaxy in the palm of his right hand.
He placed it on her ring finger, and it stayed here, hovering like a butterfly.
"What is this?" she asked.
"A gift. So... you can feel the lights' warmth wherever you are."
"It does feel warm! It is so small! But there is a part of The Void here. Will it take me?"
She peered closer at the little galaxy. At the centre, was a pinprick of very bright light.

"Where there is beauty, there is horror," said the male. "Everything has an opposite. Light and dark, hot and cold, black and white. Don't be afraid of The Void. We are light. We are its opposite."

The female touched his face. "Are you my opposite? How do you know all of this?"

He smiled. "Maybe I am your opposite. I saw it all. I saw it all begin. Come with me. Let us see this together. This new world should be celebrated."

She nodded happily and looked just once more at the blue star.

"I want to see everything with you." She looked down at the little galaxy on her finger. "Are you sure I can take this with me?" she asked the male, taking his hand.

He nodded and gestured to the world around them. "We belong here now. All of this is our home, is it not? Who do you think we need to ask permission from?"

The female thought about this. "Perhaps... The Void... no, we are all the same here. All fighting to be allowed here."

The two giants continued to wonder at their new home. The female felt a strange feeling in herself as she moved with her companion. A feeling of thankfulness that she was here and a slight feeling of fragility. Knowing The Void was trying to take the light back made her want to treasure this world even more. Travelling with the starry couple was the little galaxy. Neither of the beings realised that, within even the small galaxy, was a little solar system, and within that little solar system was a family of tiny planets.

The Solar System

Nine planets surrounded a single star, which was their Sun.

The closest planets were small and rocky, while the planets reaching away from The Sun were larger and made of gases. Radiating out from The Sun were glass arms leading each planet to it, a fragile cold orrery floating in the now vivid and electric Void. The Sun itself was baseless, following the rules of gravity; however, the planets that were connected by these bridges, just shy of reaching The Sun's surface, circled their Sun on a flat plane.

Not many other solar systems had these glass bridges, as usually they were broken up due to asteroid collisions. If a planet was too far from a star itself, the bridges would become too brittle and shatter. The remaining glass shards would float amongst the planets until they would dissipate or crumble into dust.

   Within these nine planets lived humanoids, or Heerajras. They were beings that looked like humans but with a far higher resilience to live in space and had abilities to grow and shrink as large as their home planets. Naturally, on their planets, they were about fifty thousand feet tall, give or take the varying heights and ages of the Heerajras themselves.

They were all born from their planets, without parents, and aged imperceptibly. In turn, the Heerajras could live longer, but no longer than their planets' untouched lifespan.

    As they were born from their planets, their energy source was their home; they didn't need to consume food or drink as a necessity but did so out of pleasure. There was one Heerajra per planet and one Heerajra that lived on The Sun, their Queen. The second royal member was the Heerajra that lived on The Moon. As moons were rare in this space, it was common to regard the moons as princes or princesses.

    In this particular solar system, there was one moon that was locked to the third planet from The Sun. There were only a few miles between The Moon and the planet and, because they were in such proximity, they were considered siblings.

The elder sibling was called Navas, and she was the sole inhabitant of Planet Navas. All the Heerajras named their planets after themselves, to reinforce their connection to their home.

Navas was a Heerajra and, had she been a human, would have looked around twenty-three years old. She had sage green skin and bright, almost glowing, yellow eyes. She wore an emerald flounce top that showed off her slim midriff and buxom chest, and a blue and white skirt that swayed like water to her ankles. Her white hair was bouncy, cloudlike and reached down to the back of her knees.

Her planet was a mix of grass-covered lands, trees that reached up to the sky, and oceans that lapped the shores. The greenery was scaled to her height, so she didn't tower over trees or mountains. Flowers were larger than what humans could envision on Planet Navas and were scaled to their planet's surroundings. On one half of her planet, where The Moon didn't sit above, were volcanoes, mighty spewing monsters whose lava fell into the planet's oceans creating hot steams and heavy white clouds. The sky, into which the volcanoes bellowed, was a deep crimson, weighted with granite and black ash. Navas rarely ventured to this side of her planet.

As The Moon was so close, a frozen tidal wave had risen high enough to almost scrape the underneath. The craggy ice pointed out from the ocean into a column so that, from afar, The Moon would resemble a crystal sculpture, supported by the ice stand. Part of the glass bridge was woven through this mountain of ice, but the Princess and her sister had carved part of the ice into steps.

Navas's planet was slowly settling down from its birth and, despite the outside world taking seconds to be born from The Void, millennia had passed at the same time.

The Heerajras lived in a single abode, or Kassel, on their planets, not too far from the glass bridge connection, which was usually closest to the north pole. Snow on Navas's planet fell on only the highest peaks on the mountains, but otherwise grassy banks and blue skies topped both poles of her planet. Weather change did happen on her planet, but rarely so and, when it did rain, snow or bluster, it was forceful and could end within a day or so. Seasons could last for years or end overnight.

Navas's Kassel was a half-roofed studio loft, with windows reaching from floor to ceiling to allow as much sunshine in as possible. Blank canvases were racked on heaving shelves. Jars and paintbrushes stood to be washed in a paint-strewn metal sink. She had one tiny bedroom and seating area, but rarely used it as she would spend most of her time in the studio. She did decide that, as she spent so much time in her studio, it was best to have a space to make tea.

Whatever a Heerajra desired to make could be materialised, so long as they were on their planet, as it had the same energy as themselves. Navas liked to keep her Kassel simple so that she could focus on her artwork.

One sunny day, Navas was leaning over a canvas, painting. Her brush slipped over the canvas, finishing a rainbow that dropped behind a forest. Her fingers were stained with paint and her back ached, as she had been sitting for hours. Any blank wall was filled with finished paintings, all showcasing her planet and the stars around her.

Just as Navas was reaching for another brush, her sister, the Princess of The Moon, came through to the studio. Princess Liras was around fifteen years old, with ghost-white skin and pale purple eyes. She wore a deep purple lehnga with thousands of brilliantly sparkling jewels sewn into the fabric.

    She wore many silver rings, a haath phool (rings that are linked by chains to bangles), a nose ring that was chained to her earring called a nath, and a tika that bore an almost black amethyst that dropped onto her forehead from her hair parting. She was bedecked in silver jewellery in the form of a necklace, armbands and earrings, all embedded with amethysts.

Her thick silver hair, covered by a chunni, was braided down to her ankles, and she chimed every time she walked, as her anklets had tiny silver bells attached to them. Her little pointed shoes that matched her dress poked from just underneath the silver embroidery of her dress.

"Oh! Sorry to disturb you, sister!" Princess Liras said politely and hung by the doorway. Navas, paintbrush in mouth, as she was using both hands to mix a new colour, shook her head.

"Don't be silly, I'll be done soon…" She took the paintbrush out from her mouth and stood back to scrutinise the painting.

"How is it?" she asked her sister.

Princess Liras peered over to see a photo-perfect rendition of a rainbow. "It is lovely, sister. Perhaps I can hang this one up in the palace?"

Navas smiled but didn't offer to give her the painting.

There was no space for her gaudy painting in the palace. The Princess's Kassel was a white, pearlescent palace on The Moon, with minarets and a sweeping dome at the centre. There were silk purple flags that swayed on top of the minarets, lined with gold stitching. Although the palace looked pale from the outside, inside the ceilings were decorated with pearl and lilac mosaics, with white silk sheets. The garden area, although it had no plants, had a wonderful fountain that sprayed out liquid iron.

Navas rarely visited her sister in the desolate palace. It was just too stark for her liking. Also, the palace was not supposed to be used solely to meet family. Navas was glad her sister could take a short walk on the glass bridge to visit her instead, which was almost daily.

Navas made ginkgo tea from a floral urn for her sister, who sat on the cleanest barstool she could find. Navas knew to get a clean mug for her sister but could only find a gingko-stained one. Navas hated tidying up.

"What shall we do today, sister?" she asked. "Take a walk through the woods? Swim? Or we can go to the ice mountains?"

Princess Liras looked down at her tea after noticing a pool of blue paint on the floor. She knew her sister was messy. It was as if the studio was a living painting, with new colours in new places each day. Her palace was sterile in comparison.

"I have a favour to ask you," Liras replied. "Did you know it is the Queen's birthday soon? She has nearly completed a whole orbit." Her eyes were wide.

Navas cradled her chin and smiled. "Not at all. It can't be soon, can it?"

Liras wasn't sure if Navas was teasing her, so she carried on.

"It's in about twenty Navas years, or thereabouts. See, the Queen has always reminded me when we have dinner. But, this time, I was thinking we could all get together. Us and the other Heerajras, not just the Queen and I."

Navas smiled as her sister spoke carefully. The Queen's birthday, from what she had heard from her sister, was very formal and she herself had never received an invite.

"That's a great idea! I mean, the outer Heerajras will be tricky to convince, but I think it's a nice thing to do!" Navas gulped down her tea. "What's the favour?"

Princess Liras smiled sheepishly. "Well, I would love to send invites out to our family. It's just that I was thinking of personalised invites. I was thinking of going myself, but I cannot travel from my palace overnight, so..."

"You want me to go?"

"Yes, thank you."

Navas stood and stretched out. "Wouldn't Iros make sense? She can move faster than I can."

Iros was the closest Heerajra to The Sun.

Princess Liras explained that she only trusted her sister.

Navas hauled herself onto the tabletop next to her sister. She had a think. She would rather stay at home, but this was a rare occasion to meet the other Heerajras and the Queen. Also, she didn't want to let her little sister down. "Sure, I'll do this for you, sister," said Navas. "We can't have you getting your dress all unkempt," she added playfully.

Princess Liras looked relieved. "Thank you. It means a lot to me. You'll have to go in the morning."

Navas frowned promptly. So soon? Could there be a chance to back out? She suddenly felt regret.

As if reading her mind, Princess Liras handed her sister a black silk pouch filled with amethysts. Navas fished out a purple gem and admired it in the light.

"A gift from the Princess? How can anyone refuse? It's beautiful," Navas said favourably.

The sisters went to sit out on the sunny banks outside the studio.

"When was the last time you saw everyone?" Princess Liras asked Navas.

Navas shook her head. She must have been her sister's age or younger at the time, but even then, she hadn't met everyone. She remembered Princess Liras was at least four when she told her big sister that there were others out there, that it wasn't just the three of them. The Queen had told her, so it must be true, Navas remembered a pigtailed Princess Liras proclaiming.

Navas recalled visiting Planet Leifweiden, the planet next to hers, and meeting the charming and handsome Leifweiden, who was just slightly older than her. She hadn't seen him in a long time, she felt. The outer planets hadn't been visited enough. The denizens of the planets did like to keep to themselves, Navas reasoned.

Princess Liras decided to do her sister's hair and braided it like her own, but weaved flowers into it. There was barely any space to do the same for Princess Liras, as her hair was studded with so many tiny jewels, so Navas slipped a tulip behind her ear.

Princess Liras loved the colours of Planet Navas. The orange-rust colour when the season became cooler, the whites of snow... and her favourite, when The Sun beamed down, and flowers dotted the greenery.

However, Princess Liras didn't realise how strong The Sun's reflected light was from her own mirrored moon in certain seasons, and that Navas would sometimes have to seek shelter from the brilliant hot beams as they shot onto her planet.

Navas watched Princess Liras pick flowers that only sprouted after the cold, without the aid of insects or bugs, and smiled.

    She thought back to when they had first met, when Princess Liras was still a baby. The Moon had always hung to the planet like a child and the glass bridge was always there, as far as Navas could remember. However, when Navas was aged five (in appearance), she remembered when the Queen made a fleeting visit to The Moon and, on the same day, the palace was created.

The Queen wore an impossibly long cape that fell off The Moon like a curtain of water. Young Navas snuck up to the bridge and into the cold palace, where she found a small baby wrapped in ivory silk, wailing. Navas decided that this baby needed looking after, and so she visited the baby twice a day, held her in her arms as she walked around the palace, and carefully took her to her own planet to lie on the grass in the sunshine. It wasn't until the baby had turned a year old (at least, in appearance) did the Queen visit the palace to tell Navas that the baby was a princess and her sister. Navas had only seen the Queen once more after that. Navas had never felt such responsibility for anything after this moment. The little child she had come across was now her new sister, her family.

The sisters stayed together until night began to fall and Princess Liras thanked her sister again.
"I must reach the palace now. I'll see you off in the morning."
Navas nodded and patted the pouch of amethysts in her hand. She didn't think she could back out now and said

merrily, "This is exciting. To see everyone in one place. I can't wait!"

Princess Liras looked up at the sky. It was now a deep blue, the galaxy's arm appearing from the darkness. It was a foggy, dark, smoky arm that was surrounded by sharp, sparkling stars. *Another orbit*, Liras thought admirably.

"Do we have time for a swim?" asked Liras.

Navas watched Princess Liras transform her clothes into a purple swimsuit that was studded with pearls, and a small lace skirt hung from her hips. Navas nodded and changed into a blue and green bikini. They travelled over to the nearest body of water that was hot from the falling lava and jumped in with a splash.

After swimming, playing and sloshing water at each other, they both hung from the ocean's rocky edge and enjoyed the warmth of the waters around them, their cheeks flushed. Steam clouds floated past them nonchalantly. Princess Liras closed her eyes and sighed happily.

"I need this in the palace."

"You could, Lili," Navas sighed, using Princess Liras's nickname. Princess Liras sometimes objected to that name, and other times not, depending on her mood.
"I know. It's just better here." As Princess Liras mellowed in the waters, she reached out and squeezed Navas's hand. Navas smiled over at her and sighed contentedly.
"The sky here makes the stars seem prettier," added Princess Liras, gazing out into the navy sky.
Navas nodded. It was such a clear night. It was like looking into space, uninterrupted. The Heerajras could always venture out and look beyond their atmosphere; but, in reality, they were always busy tending to their planets. Princess Liras now had her eyes closed and was hugged by the steam.

Although just the thought of the journey tired Navas, she was excited at the prospect of seeing her family and to visit their homes again. Liras would be so happy to have the entire family together. Navas then thought how she could annoy her perfectly relaxed sister, but she decided not to. Not on this occasion.

***

The morning drew over Planet Navas, and Navas herself had to be woken up by her sister, who was rocking her shoulder gently.

"You must wake up now!" Princess Liras whispered hurriedly.

Navas woke up groggily. "Oh... gee, I'm sorry." She stretched and rolled out of bed. Princess Liras stood by her face cross, and arms folded.

"You'll need to leave soon! If you leave it too late, the alignment will be all wrong."

The alignment? Navas needed tea first. "Sure," she replied. "I'll be off soon. Tea, then I'll do your thing."

Princess Liras followed her sister closely to the kitchen. "My *thing*? It's important, Navas!"

Liras refused the tea and Navas gulped her weak, hot tea in one. She gasped in appreciation.

"OK, I'm done. I'll head off now." Navas splayed her hands out.

Princess Liras nodded angrily, then her face softened. "Will you... be wearing anything else?"

Navas was wearing the same outfit she always wore, namely the green top, blue skirt and no shoes. She materialised them each night, so at least there wasn't any paint on them.

"It's just that, to see the other planets… some for the first time, perhaps something more formal?" suggested Liras.

"I want to be comfortable," replied Navas. She sounded a little whiny. "Your dress is beautiful. For a princess." She grinned at her wary little sister.

"I guess…" Liras absently spun one of her bangles around her wrist. "One day, for me, we can both wear something beautiful."

Navas feigned an offended look as she said mockingly, "My dress *is* beautiful!"

Liras smiled as she shook her head.

They both reached the staircase that left the planet.

"Sure, I could conjure something more elaborate," said Navas, "but the thought of wearing a dress like yours makes me feel itchy." The number of sparkling stones on

Princess Liras's outfit made it look like she was wearing armour. It looked so heavy and uncomfortable.

Princess Liras would stay on Planet Navas until her sister returned. It would be a long trip to visit the planets, but time wasn't hours or minutes to the Heerajras. They had lived for so long that time wasn't a worrying or pressing concept for them, only alignments. The sisters hugged, and Princess Liras noticed that Navas had the pouch of amethyst tied to her skirt on her hip. Princess Liras looked relieved.

"I wouldn't want my big sister feeling itchy," said Liras. "Although, my dress isn't itchy. But one day, we'll both wear something beautiful! If anyone says they won't come, please don't be hard on them. But try to persuade them! The planet's alignment is on the amethyst, so you won't need to remember it."

"I'll politely annoy them," said Navas. "OK. It'll be fine, sister. Don't fret."

Princess Liras unclasped her hands from her chest. She nodded determinedly. "I'll see you soon. This will be the first time we will all be together! Thank you, sister."

Navas blew her a kiss and climbed up the glass steps out of her planet. There was no turning back now. She suddenly missed her canvases and bed. She assumed her sister would give her no time to back out of this, hence the next day trip.

The sky Navas went through went from cyan to a hazy midnight blue to black. The stars suddenly popped out from around her as she was plunged into perma-night. She could see the top of The Moon, peeking out from behind her planet.

Navas was high enough to see her planet's scope and took a while to admire the greens and blues and the lava-soaked half. She wished she had brought a sketch pad and debated whether to head back down so she could capture this moment.

No, she had to focus on her task. Looking up, she could see the connecting bridge to the glass steps, and she carried on up, taking in the fresh coolness of her surroundings. She made it to the bridge. It was miles long and wide, enough to roll down an entire gas planet like a bowling ball. The glass itself sparkled and shone from the precious stones trapped inside. It was dizzying at first, despite the thickness of the bridge. Navas could still see straight through to nothingness. The Heerajras could float briefly on their planets and in space, so didn't have a fear of heights, but they could still feel off-kilter.

Navas grew to the size of her planet and started her journey. She could have floated to all the planets but wanted to walk on the cold bridge. Everything in space moved as if it were underwater and her hair floated around her. Without the guide of the bridge, it was easy to lose your bearings.

***

Princess Liras, back on Navas's home planet, sat beside the tulips and stroked one of the yellow petals. She hoped her sister stayed safe and that her family would come together.

She resisted plucking a flower from the soil and returned to her own home.

Back in her bare, undecorated palace, Liras sat in a square courtyard and nestled amongst aubergine purple bolster cushions, trimmed with a gold fringe.

She materialised a veena, a stout sitar-like instrument with a bulbous wooden curve at one end. To produce the hypnotic, reverberating sound, similar to the depth of strings deeply humming, she sat crossed-legged with the instrument across her lap and plucked and strummed the strings, going slowly and then losing herself, her hands and fingertips a rhythmic blur across the bridges. She slowed down and then played a more haunting song; one she had been practising while away from her sister.

On the day of the Queen's birthday, she wanted to play this song for the whole family. She had never even mentioned this to Navas and couldn't wait to perfect the song for her. Princess Liras was filled with trepidation, wondering how the others would be with her sister. She paused for a moment, took a deep breath and continued her practice.

The Planets

The first planet Navas wanted to visit was Planet Iros. Navas would have to pass Planet Celd Dion, a yellow, gas-covered rock and the second planet from The Sun. It was easier to go in planet order, she reasoned.

Planet Iros was the closest planet to The Sun. It was a small, bare world that was covered in black granite sand that glittered when the burning Sun hit the surface. To avoid being in the sunshine for too long, Iros's Kassel was located underneath the surface, the roof barely peeking out from the sands. It was a large, iron-floored room that had hundreds of disco balls hanging from the ceiling, and a bar that held bubbling and strange cocktails in heavy diamond decanters.

      Iros was a teenager, who looked around seventeen. She had jet-black skin and brilliant white hair, styled in massive flicks and curls that cascaded from her crown to her collar bones. She wore a sequinned white mini dress with white, knee-high platform boots. Her dress would illuminate when caught in The Sun's rays.

Her hooped earrings were as large as bangles and her hands were ornamented with silver rings, tipped with a turquoise manicure.

Navas descended onto the planet from the stairs that led from the glass bridge. The stairs took the visitor to the home Kassel of the Heerajra. As well as the planet's energy, the Heerajras also had a unique energy coding. Heerajras could feel each other's energy, so you would know, if you paid attention, that someone else was on your planet, without being anywhere near the north pole.

The Heerajras didn't tend to stray too far from their Kassels, and each Kassel was built around the size of the Heerajra. The planet's occupants rarely became their planet's size, unless they were out in the solar system. Abodes that were built to scale could become looming buildings to smaller Heerajras, and even larger still, as the planet increased in size. Navas could scale herself relative to the rockier planets she was visiting – although, compared to the gas giants, there wasn't any way she could grow to reach the same size as the giant Heerajras, as everyone was limited to their planet's size.

Navas hoped everyone would be easily found at their Kassels.

Navas stepped down onto Planet Iros and her feet sank into the cool sands. It was quiet on this planet and the sky was black, with constant night, unlike on her own planet. The Sun appeared much larger here compared to her shores, but the planet was decidedly cool. Navas didn't understand why and reasoned it was The Sun holding its energy back for Iros.

  She found the door to Iros's Kassel and entered a dark-lit staircase, with neon graffiti patterning the walls. Navas found Iros reclining over a leather bar couch, sunglasses awry and silver streamers tossed over her. An empty glass hung miraculously from her fingertips. Navas gently shook Iros awake and was met with a scream.

"Navas? What are you doing here?"

Navas grinned. "Good morning. Long night?"

Iros heaved herself upright and pressed her head.

"Yeah... it was fun, though."

She pulled the streamers off herself. Navas was curious about Iros. She didn't think anyone else was invited to her parties, yet she knew Iros held one every night and played music from a little machine on the bar counter. Navas had never received an invite from Iros.

Because she liked to party, Iros had a habit of blocking out The Sun by her blacked-out Kassel and sunglasses. Nevertheless, the Queen and Iros did get on, from what Navas had heard from Iros herself and Liras. Navas had met Iros more times than the other Heerajras, as Princess Liras and Iros were close in age and relationship. However, Iros had never been to the palace on The Moon.

Iros stood to get a drink and offered one to Navas, who refused. Iros's heels clicked over the iron floor as she went behind her bar and Navas perched on an iron barstool. Navas watched as Iros downed a wonderfully shimmering blue liquid in one hit.

"Oh, I feel better now," drawled Iros. "Long time no see? How are you?"

Navas nodded and explained what Princess Liras was requesting. A gathering for the Queen's birthday.

"Oh, that's cool," said Iros. "You think the outer Heerajras would bother? Geadeous probably won't." Planet Geadeous was the fifth planet from The Sun and Geadeous herself was a glamorous and proud woman.
"I've been asked to get everyone together." Navas said this happily, but Iros pouted.
"Good luck with that."
Navas remembered the amethysts and placed one on the bar. "It's not a bribe. More like a please and thank you?"
Iros lowered her sunglasses on her nose and stared at the amethyst. Her irises were a pale silver.
"Wow, your sister must be serious. To offer a gem from The Moon." Iros carefully lifted it. "I'll be there, Navas. Just don't bank on the others coming. I have to go, don't I? I'm sure the Queen will notice if I'm not there."
Navas thanked her. "It'll mean a lot to my sister."
"I can bring drinks! That'll help the whole day." The girls both looked up as The Sun shone through a very small square in the ceiling, lighting up the disco balls. Iros's dress lit up, too, as she poured another drink.

"We should visit you more often." Navas was captivated by the dancing lights as they bounced from the disco balls and sparkling bottles.

"Feel free to," said Iros. "Princess Liras does."

"You can come to see us both on Planet Navas."

Iros dropped the amethyst into an empty champagne glass. "Maybe... no offence, but your planet is kinda... boring. Like, it's nice, but there's like... no atmosphere."

Navas narrowed her eyes at Iros playfully.

"After the birthday party, we'll come here."

Iros smiled and said seriously, "Please do, but dress up. Like, Princess Liras looks amazing, and you need some sparkle." She leant over the bar and lowered her glasses again. "Bring shoes, too."

Navas bit her lip, then replied sarcastically, "Sure, you get the drinks ready, and I'll bring shoes. You know Liras is a princess, that's why she looks so decorated."

Iros pressed her sunglasses back up her nose. "Yeah, and you're her sister, so make an effort." She tipped the amethyst out of the champagne glass onto her palm.

Navas patted her own hair down. "There, as much effort as you'll get from me." She was not taking Iros seriously at all, but Navas had such bad delivery with humour that no one could ever tell.

She stood to leave and Iros followed her out to the surface.

"Ugh, I've not been out since... I don't know." Iros made a visor with her hand, despite wearing sunglasses.

Navas looked down to see that her feet were blackening from the sand. *Maybe I shouldn't visit the others dressed this way?* she thought.

Iros had the amethyst in her hand and playfully threw it in the air to catch it, but it fell into the black sand and was camouflaged. The girls froze.

"Navas, what a piece of hiss! Help me find it!"

"Iros, I need to visit everyone today!" Navas backed away towards the glass bridge.

"Navas, *please*. I'll never get another one!"

Iros went on her hands and knees and Navas reluctantly joined her.

"Oh, I'm too drunk for this!" Iros wailed.

The girls' fingers dug and burrowed into the blackness, Iros's long, blue nails getting sandier by the minute. She pulled out a large rock she thought was the amethyst, but it was a lump of granite.

"Maybe we're making it worse, and it's gotten deeper?" Navas said unhelpfully, to wind Iros up.

Iros ignored her and began to panic. The black sand was now reaching her elbows. She cocked her head up to look at Navas desperately.

"Help me look, or I'll tell the Queen!"

Navas had to laugh. Seeing the usually glacial cool Iros overreact made her smile.

"Ok, ok, calm down. We'll find it." She grabbed Iros's arm and slowly moved it away from the sand.

Iros took a moment to calm down and, gently, Navas combed through the sand to find the dark purple gem. She stood up in victory.

Iros grinned and Navas saw that her teeth had little grey crystals embedded in them.

"Thanks, Navas," said Iros. "I can't lose it – I'd never get another one!"

Navas looked at the sandy amethyst in her palm. To her, Princess Liras was her sister first and then the Princess. Of course, the others would see her as the Princess, first and foremost, and then as a relation to Navas.

"It's ok," she replied softly, handing over the amethyst. "Take care of it, ok?" Iros nodded gratefully. However, by the time Iros had reached her Kassel door, she had lost the amethyst again.

"*Navas!*" she whined.

Navas shook her head in mock scolding. "You need to stop drinking!"

"Just help me!" Iros bit back.

Navas managed to find the amethyst for Iros, who went back to her home "for a much-needed drink".

Navas, back on the glass bridge, brushed off as much sand as she could. There was black sand under her nails and speckling her sleeves. Even her hair had managed to sweep it up. She'd spent too long shaking and dusting and realised she had to move on. She was sure no one would notice how grainy she had become. Navas looked out in the direction of the other planets and tried to think positively. It would be nice to see her family. She didn't need a tea just yet.

***

The next Heerajra she needed to visit was Celd Dion. Celd Dion looked like he was around fifty years old and wore a yellow tweed suit over an orange waistcoat. His suit was highlighted with specks of gold and orange trim, with a star-shaped orange and black flower in his lapel. His polished mahogany brown leather Oxford shoes matched his leather gloves. He had pale, straw-coloured hair, and his lip was topped by a flicked-up moustache. His skin was also a pale yellow, barely distinguishable from his hair. His thin, angry eyes were an emerald green, the only green on his entire planet.

    He was a gardener and grew spiky, jet-black plants and corn all over his planet. The black crops were a sharp contrast to the yellow mustard colourings of the planet. The sky was heavy with yellow smoke; pools of acid dotted the land and a thick, choking, cloying smell permeated the air.

He carried a brass pocket watch covered in symbols that none of the other Heerajras could comprehend, and smoked pipes, cigarettes and cigars that added yet more smoke and ash to his noxious surroundings.

His Kassel was a refinery plant, built of copper and brass. Plants would be woven through the machinery to be turned into a thick black oil that was, in turn, used to water the crops.

Navas stood at the top of the stairs reaching down to the yellow, smoggy planet. The stairs narrowed down to a Heerajra's size from the planet-wide opening of the bridge, so she leant against the cool banister as she stepped down. The stairs led a step or two away from the planet; they didn't quite connect, to allow for planet rotation and orbiting.

Celd Dion didn't seem to get on with Navas, either because of her age, her being a woman, or maybe even her hair. Navas didn't know why and had only ever met him once, on top of his bridge. It didn't go well.

She stepped down the glass staircase slowly, the air becoming heavier and thicker, her lungs quickly filling with the smog from the top layer of the atmosphere. Soon, she could see the surface of the planet and her eyes began to water, and her breathing became constricted. The heat of the planet made her sage skin shine from sweat. Everything looked yellow to her, a hazy yellow fog that was barely interrupted by mountains or hills.

She could see Celd Dion watering the plants near his Kassel, and she had to wade through miles of high, black corn to meet him.
"Celd Dion, it's Navas," she called out once she reached him.
He didn't bother turning around. "What is it, girl?"
Navas resisted taking offence.
"My— The Princess is inviting you to a gathering for the Queen."
Celd Dion stopped watering and waited for the next line.

"So, it's the Queen's birthday and the— Princess Liras thought that—"

"Just spit it out!"

Navas thought it was a good idea to take a deep breath, and so she took in a massive gulp of the toxic air. She began to cough loudly and found she couldn't stop. The more she tried to suppress the cough, the louder it became. Now her eyes were streaming. She held up her hand to reassure Celd Dion that she was OK, but he just stared back at her impatiently.

"Sorry, just take this—" Navas handed Celd Dion the amethyst and he snatched it, as if he'd catch a plague from her.

"The Queen's birthday." Celd Dion, ignoring the spluttering Navas, was honoured. The Queen was everything Navas wasn't. Mature, dignified and well dressed. He could never understand how the Princess's joint planet was so... unkempt. The Queen had less sand on her, for one thing.

Navas didn't look her best in the humidity, as her hair was now twice the volume. Her eyes were watering, and her cheeks were a dark green from her coughing.

"Tell the Princess I will be honoured to join her in this gathering," clipped Celd Dion.

Navas wiped her face with her sleeve and swallowed a cough. "Thank you," her voice cracked. "She will be grateful. Pleased…" Navas couldn't stay any longer in this atmosphere.

Celd Dion held on to the amethyst in his gloved hand, while Navas's ample chest was heaving from the coughing fit.

"We're done here, girl," he said curtly. "You can go now."

Navas wished she could throw an ear of corn at him, but she remained calm for the sake of her sister. She watched as Celd Dion pop open a black umbrella after cradling his hand towards his sky. Navas looked up. The smog and heavy, lumbering clouds above them made it appear as though the clouds were falling towards Celd Dion's planet.

As she took a second to admire it, a drop of acidic rain fell on her cheek, making her wince.

"Be off, girl…" Celd Dion sought refuge in his Kassel, so Navas rushed through the black corn to the stairs, evading most of the rain.

When she reached the bridge, she lay down on her back and gave a deep sigh.
Of course, Celd Dion wanted her to get drenched with acid. She was relieved that she wouldn't have to see that man for another twenty years now. Navas closed her eyes and breathed in the cool air around her, deep breaths that made her chest rise and fall. She peered over to watch the yellow clouds scud across the gas-choked planet and, for a moment, wondered if Celd Dion ever went up and out of his own planet to enjoy this coolness. Navas tried to tame her floating hair back down with her palms.

Turning her head, Navas saw the next planet in the distance, Planet Leifweiden.
In comparison to Celd Dion's planet, where clouds prevented the sunlight from seeping through, Planet

Leifweiden was cold, snow-covered and had the darkest green fir trees that resembled her own trees back home. Navas was now covered in black sand and sweat, and her hair refused to deflate.

She'd passed her own planet to get to Planet Leifweiden and watched as The Moon was rippled with light from the ocean bouncing off The Sun's rays. As much as she wanted to jump home to bathe in the ocean waters, she decided to continue. Princess Liras had timed the invites, so the planets were relatively aligned to make her journey easier.

  Navas hadn't seen Leifweiden for about five of her own years. She walked down the glass steps a little and grew closer to his stark white planet. She sat on the glass step and rested her elbows on her knees, enjoying watching the skating, powdery snow across the plains pushed by the howling winds.

She was excited to see Leifweiden and nervous at the same time. She would feel giddy seeing him, yet completely relaxed and calm. She smiled and her cheeks warmed up from the thought of him. She stood up and felt the amethyst-filled pouch on her hip. *For Princess Liras*, she thought quietly. *It's the only reason I am here.* Navas arrived on Planet Leifweiden. The snow was shin high, a calming blue as if reflecting the sky above it. Gusts of wind blew the snow around Navas, and she was glad for the cool effect it had.

Leifweiden's planet was dark, and the giant fir trees were pitch black in the night. Navas felt inspired artistically when she saw just how black they were, with not a single needle reflecting a photon of light.
He lived in a fortress, the dark trunks of the trees making up the walls. There were small arrow slits in the walls that lit up from the candles inside, and a watchtower above that housed a swaying bell. Navas didn't see him until she got closer to the watchtower, where he was hunched over a telescope.

She smiled. Leifweiden could see out for miles but had no idea she was even on his planet. Navas gathered up snow into a ball and threw it, aiming at his back. The snowball sailed through an arrow slit and knocked an object over inside. Navas gasped loudly, then covered her mouth with her hand.

Leifweiden jumped up and spun around, peering out to see who it was. Smiling, he rushed down and lowered the bridge to allow access into his Kassel.

"Navas! Long time no see!" he yelled happily over the winds and, when they reached each other, he hugged her hard, so they spun around. "Come in," he said. "This is a light storm, but it'll only get worse."

Leifweiden was a stocky man, a few years older in appearance to Navas, and had dark navy hair that brushed over his forehead and nape. He was wrapped in a dark blue scarf, and he wore a fur-lined, sky-blue tunic, brown trousers, with heavy fur-lined tan snow boots. Tawny leather, fingerless gloves encased his hands. His ice-blue eyes stood out from his pale grey skin, and they almost glowed in the darkness.

Navas had always considered him to be a striking-looking man and so kind. As much as Heerajras were anatomically correct, and could enjoy being in a couple, there wasn't a possibility of living on another planet that could support them indefinitely.

The chances of finding a planet that had the same energy and beat as their own, enough to sustain them, was infinitesimally small. Two Heerajras couldn't reproduce, and the planet's inhabitants didn't savour time, but knew there was an eventual end to their long lives, as seen in their altering homes. This was calmly accepted. As they didn't have the biological means to reproduce, nor was it in their makeup to continue a bloodline, a Heerajra didn't look for a romantic partner out of need.

Despite this, Heerajras had the desire to be romantically involved. Leifweiden and Navas knew that they had a connection and wanted to see each other more, but both knew he couldn't be a distraction to the Princess's sister. Neither had ever told the other out loud about their attraction, and Navas was unsure if she could ever be romantically involved with Leifweiden and still be there for her sister.

Knowing Princess Liras, she wouldn't have minded either way.

As close as Navas was to the Princess, she didn't know what the Queen would say at all, or whether the Queen would be happy about Navas's attention being diverted away from her younger, royal sibling.

Leifweiden led Navas into a large hall that had a fire burning. Rugs, woven in geometric patterns, were laid out on the floor, and a few were hung up on the stone walls as tapestries. She suddenly felt comfortable here and sat on a wooden bench that was piled with thick, grey throws. Leifweiden wrapped one of the throws around her tightly and went to make a hot drink, a pine needle tea. Navas cradled the mug once it was passed to her. Leifweiden then asked after Princess Liras.

"She is fine, that's why I'm here," replied Navas. "It's the Queen's birthday and she'd like us all to be there." She handed Leifweiden an amethyst that had the alignment date carved into it and he took it gratefully.

"The Princess should know that I don't need a gift to encourage me to go," he said. "I'd be honoured."

"Everyone is going to be invited..." said Navas. "I have just been to visit Celd Dion, but he was *prickly* as always."

"He's ok with me..." replied Leifweiden. "When did I see him last…? A few years ago, it must be." He was staring into the gem.

"Because you're a man, I think," Navas said disparagingly.

"Most likely. So, are you going to see Geadeous next? I wish you luck." Leifweiden gave her a roguish smile. Navas smiled playfully back at him and tried to pull her skirt over her toes as she sat with her knees to her chest. Geadeous was a feisty woman.

"I will need it," she said. "It's been nice seeing everyone in a way…" Navas stood up and went over to the fireplace. The flames licked and flicked, and she was mesmerised. Leifweiden watched her. She was so beautiful to him. Her glowing eyes, long white hair and the sense of joy around her. All he ever wanted to do was hug her when he saw her.

He went over and placed the amethyst on the mantelpiece in front of Navas and she jumped. They were close together and he placed his hand very gently on her back.

"It's so warm," she murmured.

Realising their proximity, they both blushed and took a step away from each other.

"What have you seen then, Leifweiden?" Navas asked her voice high. "There must be something *wonderful* in the sky."

Navas was smiling, but he couldn't return the smile. They went to the brick watchtower with the lone, swinging bell, and she could hardly move for the many blueprints and the limited space. There was a telescope pointing up to the stars, a chair and a tiny table bowed by the weight of the blueprints.

Navas became aware of Leifweiden's chest pressing on her back.

"Oh my, it's cosy here," she laughed.

She'd taken the throw, and he pulled it around her again. As Leifweiden did this, she noticed his sleeves were tinged red. It looked like he had watery paint stains creeping up his arms, rather than a fabric colouring.

"What are these for?" she asked, indicating to the copious blueprints scattered around the lookout.

Leifweiden adjusted the telescope, his arms over her shoulders.

"I'm building," he said. "Can you see the volcano? It's dead, unlike those of your planets. I want to hollow it out and create an observatory. I know the Queen can see as far as she can, but I want to help. I want to know what is out there, too, you know?"

Navas nodded and touched the gold telescope carefully. "Do you... use this to watch us?"

Leifweiden looked down at her and grinned. "Of course, I watch you every day," he lied.

"I wouldn't be able to stop. I'd be so nosy!" she admitted.

"I may glance at our neighbours, but I'd feel... intrusive," said Leifweiden. "It's better to meet people face to face."

Navas nodded and felt her cheeks grow hot. He was so close to her.

"We really should see each other more," he said sternly. "It's easy to get preoccupied. Strange how we're all neighbours and yet very much strangers." Navas didn't know if he meant the pair of them or the other Heerajras.

She touched his hand that was resting on the telescope and said gently, "What did you want to show me?"

Leifweiden gestured out to space.

He sat down on the chair behind the telescope, then indicating to Navas to sit on his lap. As she did so, he wrapped his arms around her waist, softened by the throw.

In the distance, through the telescope, Navas could see a faint red light.

"What is that?"

"I don't know, darling. It's been there for a long time. It came out of nowhere." He was worried, pensive. Navas took another look through the telescope. It was a strong, red light with a slight blur around the edge.

"Maybe a galaxy. Or a dying star," said Leifweiden. The Heerajras had witnessed a star exploding, and its light lit up their skies for weeks.

"Will you tell the Queen?" asked Navas.

He nodded. "I will. I'm sure she can see it. It may disappear in that time, perhaps."

Leifweiden sounded so concerned that she just wanted to hug him and nestle into his chest. She turned to face him and placed a hand on his cheek. He looked disquieted.

"It's nothing. It'll go soon," he replied with little conviction.

He looked out to the sky and frowned.

"I have to finish that observatory." He turned in his seat to examine a blueprint and Navas nearly fell off his lap.

"Sorry! Oh, my goodness – I just had an idea!"

"I can leave—" She sat on the creaking little table.

"Oh no, you can stay," rushed Leifweiden.

Navas was sitting on a blueprint that he needed, and she said between moving so he could reach his papers, "I need to see everyone as soon as possible."

Leifweiden stopped and tilted his head. "I'm sorry, sweet." He held her fingertips. "I've been a bit distracted. The light... and seeing you. Don't leave it so long." In the close quarters, it was so easy to fall into an embrace, but they both let the electricity between them disperse.

"It'll be OK," said Navas smiling. "Once we all meet up, everyone will want to see each other more."

They left the watchtower and went back to the main living room.

"You can keep that," teased Leifweiden. Navas realised she was still wearing the throw, now dusted with snow.

"I would love to, but not for travelling," replied Navas half laughing. "I'd ruin it somehow." She turned to look at the sky and then back at Leifweiden, who, in the reflection of the window, was writing on his ungloved palm with a heavy fountain pen. She smiled and looked back up at the deep night sky. He couldn't resist the wonder of what was out there. So many questions unanswered. So many questions you didn't know to ask, as you didn't know what you wanted to know. As she looked up, she wondered if there was ever a daytime on this white planet.

She slipped the throw off and touched his arm gently.

"Thank you. I'll see you soon."

"Navas… Wait."

Just go, she thought. *Don't get in his way.*

"Honestly, you're busy. I'll see you soon."

She left him, his arm outstretched, hastily.

Closing his smudged hand into a fist, Leifweiden sighed. That wasn't how he wanted to leave things. His heart healed and ached when she was around. But he had to finish off the observatory. Once he knew what the red light was, he'd relax. Leifweiden smiled sadly and felt dejected.

Navas couldn't have stayed longer, he reasoned. He opened his fist, and his palm was blue with smeared ink. He scoffed gently. He hoped he could remember what he had written, but his thoughts were only of Navas.

Navas reached the glass bridge and looked up in the direction of the red light. She couldn't see it from where she was, but she thought perhaps it was a dying star. She'd learnt a lot from Princess Liras, who, in turn, was enlightened by the Queen. She gazed back down at the snowy world and placed her hand on her chest.
She wanted to see more of him... maybe she could let the Queen know of her feelings. Although she felt it, deep inside, it didn't seem the right time now. Maybe when Princess Liras was older? Navas closed her eyes and took a deep breath. She didn't want to leave Leifweiden in such a rush, but he was busy... She placed a finger on her lip and closed her eyes.

The stars around her shone and sparkled and she enjoyed just being out in the solitude, if only for a moment. *Carry on*, she told herself.

The next planet was Planet Geadeous, a large red gas planet that was further out in their solar system.
Navas continued her walk.
The Sun was becoming smaller as she approached the large, looming planet.
The gas bands trailed around the planet slowly, but morphed and twisted so that they resembled liquid.
Navas had never been to Planet Geadeous but had met Geadeous on the bridge twice before.
She was in awe of the massive beast planet.

As she neared the planet, the hair on her arms began to stand on end and the air was thicker somehow. She reached the steps that led to the planet and immediately felt the pull of the giant. She carefully stepped down as the atmosphere of the planet crackled deep with energy and electricity.

From the top of the stairs within the planet, the starry sky vanished and deep orange clouds, the size of mountains, appeared. Booms of light flashed in the clouds that provided a brief light source for Navas. The winds were strong, and the smell of rust filled the air. From a distance, she could see a storm as it flashed and swirled violently. Everything was so kinetic, like a moving, living painting. And everything was larger still. The clouds seemed solid in their mass, like carved rock, mutating and rippling from the ever-moving wind. Navas had forgotten just how unstill this planet was. The lightning forks she saw were brilliant, too, as they sparked from a height, and some landed far too close to her on the stairs. The growl of thunder trembled over the planet.

Navas had seen and been in storms before, but the sounds here were amplified, and she gripped the banister of the glass steps for security.

It took her an age to walk down the steps, surrounded by the craggy cloud structures and, as she reached closer to the planet's core, the pressure increased further. Her body felt heavier, and her joints felt like they were creaking from the weight. Closer still, she could see gold pylons reaching to a building that was so large, it stood out like a cliff face amongst the bronze and terracotta clouds. In a strange way, the clouded, melting planet had an odd beauty to it. Navas felt as if she could watch the forceful, morphing clouds for ever, if it hadn't been for the heavy weight around her very being.

The building that was Geadeous's Kassel looked like a mansion. It was made of marble, and it was studded with rubies and diamonds. It was massive, from the doors to the windows, all in stretched, inflated proportions. The mansion appeared to be floating in the clouds, but there was a path, not quite on solid ground, but heavier cloud, that went past tall gold gates. The gates opened automatically when she reached them and Navas passed fountains that spurted out liquid helium. Gilded marble statues poured out the same liquid from their highest points. The statues were formless, captured sweeps of wind that had become stuck and petrified into marble.

Navas entered the mansion and, as she did so, Geadeous appeared dramatically at the top of a curved grand staircase and stepped elegantly down. She looked forty, was around a hundred feet tall and wore red robes over a silk slip that moved and waved like the bands of gas on her planet. She moved so lightly on this planet, more akin to walking on air than in the tar-thick atmosphere.

Geadeous had orange skin, very red lips and terracotta eyes. She had thick, red hair that ebbed and flowed. She also wore a lot of gold jewellery, which clinked as she moved, on her upper arms, wrists, fingers and thighs, that appeared to be a cross between decoration and armour, all pressed in with rubies. It made Navas fidgety to look at her, as she personally never wore jewellery. Geadeous's bright red silk slip trailed off into a long cape, competing against a shrug she wore that swooped from her forearms.

She was easy to visually admire, and Geadeous was her own number one fan.

    Navas observed many paintings of Geadeous, and they were picture-perfect, with Geadeous winning battles in an army of helmeted Heerajras, wearing her famous armour that was similar to a gold-plated skater dress, her hair twisted into a long braid.

She couldn't look more different today, however.

"Navas, darling! So good to see you!" She shimmied down the stairs and Navas forgot how tall Geadeous was. Geadeous hugged her and Navas was lost in her ample cleavage. Geadeous matched Navas in height as best she could. However, such was her frame, Geadeous was still considerably taller than Navas.

"Let's drink," said Geadeous keenly. "Iros has brought plenty of concoctions."

Iros is here? thought Navas crabbily. Iros would never use her speed unless it benefited her. Iros would have given out the invitations a lot faster than herself! Geadeous took Navas into a massive living room, with a mural on the ceiling depicting intertwining Heerajras in a battle. Everything was gold lined and wonderfully opulent.

Geadeous's mansion was very close to resembling a palace. If only the owner's attitude was more… refined. On a velvet seat was Iros, who looked child sized in the seat, happily drunk.

"Navas! I haven't seen you in a long time. How's the invite going?"

Navas glanced at Geadeous, who seemed to know why she was there. There was a rumble of thunder and the windowpanes rattled, their purpose of keeping the weather out strongly tested. Navas frowned slightly. From their vantage point, as the mansion was floating among sunset-rocking clouds, it made for an unsteady feeling in her stomach.

Navas needed an immobile view to steady her nausea.

"Let's drink first," said Geadeous. She poured out a vivid-blue drink and Navas thanked her hesitantly.

"So, have you seen the others? Will they be going?" Geadeous asked her.

"Not from here – I'm going in order," replied Navas. "So, I've seen Celd Dion – he was as polite as ever – and then Leifweiden…"

The two others smiled because Navas blushed slightly.

"And now you're here."

Navas nodded. "Princess Liras has asked me to invite everyone on behalf of the Queen."

"I have to go – I'm sure I'll get a scolding if I don't go," said Iros. "But… I wanna see everyone. It's been so long…" She sounded quite drunk now. She looked so relaxed here, legs resting up on the armrest, a glass that was never empty.

Geadeous smiled serenely. "So, you want me to go as well?"

A loud crash of thunder shook the palace.

Navas gulped and nodded.

"I cannot see the star you worship from here," said Geadeous. Her voice became precise. "Neither can Polymir, Crooked Dancer or Entanerus. I think it's a bright star, isn't it?"

Navas and Iros had heard this all before. Planet Geadeous was a massive planet and she decided that it was large and bright enough for her to be considered the ruler of, minimally, the second half of the solar system. As Navas was close to Princess Liras and the royal side of the planets, she felt she had to defend the Queen, and she believed the solar system shouldn't be split.

"Please come, Geadeous. Princess Liras would love to see you."

Geadeous finished her drink. "I'd like to see the Princess, but that Glaruntia…your 'Queen'. As soon as you landed, I could feel the tension in you, Navas. Do I frighten you?"

Navas shook her head and smiled happily. "You don't scare me! But I was worried you'd say no—"

"I am not going."

"Please, don't go for the Queen, but for my sister. Here." Navas produced the amethyst and Geadeous's eyes widened.

Iros smiled at her reaction.

"From The Princess?" Geadeous took the amethyst from Navas and was silenced. Geadeous *loved* gemstones. "She's... she must be serious," she added. "Why is she so intent?" It wasn't usual for matter from other planets to be passed around, except for foods and drinks.

Navas smiled. "Because Liras loves us all. She wants to see everyone together. It's not a bad thing. This... feeling you have can be put aside for my sister."

Geadeous was still staring at the amethyst in awe.

Navas swallowed hard. There was a lot of pressure on this planet... she could feel her stomach turn.

"Do you have room for this amethyst?" Iros asked Geadeous.

"Oh, this precious stone will have a place."

Navas was cheered. "Will you come?" She could feel her forehead perspire.

Geadeous stood and gazed out at her sky from the window. "I don't want my feelings to be ignored. I can make a stand for Glaruntia... many times have I thought to venture to her and say... you are not my Queen. But I want her to come to *me*. Why should I be the one to visit *her*?"

Her voice became quiet.

Navas stood next to Geadeous and looked up to face her. "Your feelings do matter."

Geadeous pushed Navas's hair away from her face.

Navas's eyes shone as bright as polished gold.

"I must be an enemy to you, and your precious Queen," said Geadeous disdainfully.

Navas glanced at Iros, who was watching them meditatively.

She shook her head. Stepping back, Navas examined the magnificent paintings. Geadeous had her long red hair swept back, wielding an iron sword. She looked twenty years younger.

Iros joined them. "Say... tell us about the fight you had, Geadeous. It's my favourite story."

Geadeous nodded and began her story. "It was when I was younger. Before you arrived. The solar system was quieter, when it had less energy. And, one quiet day, meteorites began to rain down towards us. So, I changed into battle armour and, with my sword in hand, knocked away each meteorite. Something inside told me I had to fight. An instinct."

Her eyes were shining from the memory. "The solar system was saved. But the meteorites didn't stop coming. Like a shower of rocks and ice," she said simply.

Iros clapped and jumped up giddily. "Without you, we'd all be in much more trouble!" A howl of wind shot past the mansion.

Navas smiled at Geadeous dolefully, who looked very proud. It was a shame she couldn't be happy with her protector status. She needed just that much more. Navas continued to observe the paintings on the ceiling. She saw a fanged woman with pitch-black skin, vibrant blood-red hair and sharp, amber eyes, as bright as lamps.

She looked manic, feral and powerful, with heavy muscles and strong hands. She was tackling meteorites and asteroids.

Geadeous and Iros both looked up alongside Navas and followed her gaze.

"My tyrant form," explained Geadeous. "When I lose my... control."

"Oh my, thank goodness you're here. We'd all be floating rocks, otherwise," Iros said, slightly slurred.

"How can a monster be our protector?"

Geadeous took a quick, agitated breath. Navas wondered if she'd ever change to her tyrant form again. She wondered if they all could become monsters. Large, unthinking beasts. She couldn't imagine the beautiful Geadeous ever being this violent. Loud, but not violent.

"I'll go, Navas. To see your sister. And I'll tell Glaruntia what I feel. I want my voice to be heard."

This was the best she'd get, Navas realised. Of course, she didn't want the Queen to be embarrassed, but, at the same time, she knew the Queen wasn't going to accept being spoken to in any disrespectful way.

She could hear a hum in her ears that was getting louder, and she wanted to leave for the bridge. A soft headache began to form across her temple.

"Thank you. It'll mean a lot to my sister." Navas smiled gratefully at Geadeous.

Iros sighed. "Now that's over, can we drink? Tell us more about your fights." Navas smiled at Iros, who was entranced by Geadeous. She was a strong, powerful woman. A defender for the solar system. Maybe you had to get drunk to handle this planet. They all sat down in the armchairs and Geadeous decanted more stories. As she did so, a massive lightning bolt stabbed the planet that made Iros and Navas jump. The mansion shuddered and a heavy fizz of static filled the air.

Both Iros and Navas were breathless for a second.

"Oh ladies," Geadeous laughed. "You're all welcome here but stay strong. This planet isn't for the weak." Navas agreed with her. It began to rain diamonds, small fragments of ice-clear stones falling into the bronze clouds.

Iros, who never had rain on her planet, ran to the window to watch. Iros suddenly reminded Navas of her inquisitive little sister. What made Geadeous want more from her home? It was just as powerful and beautiful as she was, Navas reasoned, and she watched the diamond rain spill and tumble over the planet.

The rain eventually subsided and Navas hoped she wasn't running too late, alignment-wise. She left Iros and Geadeous to gossip, assuming their drinks would run out eventually.

Climbing up the now diamond-covered stairs and back out on the bridge, Navas wondered if Geadeous was planning anything else, other than to confront the Queen. She thought that it would have been harder to convince Geadeous to go, but she seemed to want to use the dinner as an opportunity to speak her mind.

The Sun, their Queen. She was not malevolent. She wasn't tyrannical. She was their Sun. Her light shone out across the solar system, be it beating down on Planet Iros or just reaching out to Planet Entanerus.

Geadeous had enough power to rule over the solar system, Navas realised... no. She had enough *desire* for

power. Navas wondered if the other neighbours wanted to be ruled by Geadeous. The Queen had the power to rule, such was her energy. She was kind, too. *I'm sure she won't cause a scene*, thought Navas. *Geadeous has had a whole history of fighting…*
Navas could barely convince herself.
She passed the crackling and stormy planet.

The next planet she was to visit was another gas planet, a soft sandy-coloured world she had only been to once before. Navas had been much younger when she had seen the other planets, and visited Planet Goston, the eighth planet, with Princess Liras a few times.
She'd never been to Planet Crooked Dancer, the seventh planet. The Queen had suggested, a long time ago, that it would be best if she didn't visit alone. The Queen didn't visit planets much, to Navas's recollection. Her cape alone would fall off a planet's edge as it was as long as the solar system.

Navas was almost done with her task. There were only four more Heerajras to visit and then she could get home. It had been a long trip for her. She turned to observe The Sun. It was, indeed, a big star now, and she smiled at a little fleck of bright light that must have been The Moon.

It shone so brightly. Navas had no idea how long she had been walking or how long she had been on each planet. There was no setting Sun to tell her a day had passed, no darkness, no dawn.

She sat on the bridge and looked out at the expanse of space. Her atmosphere hid a lot of stars. The Kings and Queens of their world. She wondered if the other Heerajras in the solar systems got on. If they had princes rather than a princess. If they had warriors. She floated up and rested on the barrier side, her chin on her arms. Her world was beautiful. She was sure Princess Liras wanted to celebrate this and thought to take her to the planets after the celebration.

She stretched her arms up and high and made her way to Planet Polymir, the sixth planet.

Navas walked down the glass stairs from the bridge to the surface of the planet and frowned. She'd remembered the planet differently. She was sure that there was a different tone back then. She recalled blue skies, not a sepia one, and the giant trees used to have deep blue leaves on them. But now, everything had a sandy wash to it. The forests on this planet that used to mirror her own forests were now stark and the ground was drier, sandier. Her feet sank into the soft material, but it moved like a sponge, not enough resistance like ground, nor soft enough like sand.

It was quiet.

The wind ran past her softly, almost purposefully, and it felt like figures rushing past her. As Navas took a step, she heard a caw and froze. She'd not heard a noise like that before. The air was cool and incredibly light, the same lightness as a blue morning back at home.

Walking tentatively through the woods, the tonal colours shifted around her. They would phase from being sepia to monochromatic. She stopped to rub her eyes. She could see Polymir's Kassel in the distance, through a clearing in the woods. It was a slim, black, gothic building, with tiny windows. A weathervane was topped by a torn black feather. Navas watched the Kassel change from black and white to sepia, along with the planet.

It was so different from when she'd last seen this world. She called out Polymir's name. From memory, he was an older man who wore a black doublet and deep red hoses that matched his breeches and sleeves, and around his neck he wore a deep purple lace jabot.

Navas remembered that he'd had no idea what to say to the excited girl that once visited him. She remembered his pointed, burgundy beard and long, wavy hair that brushed his jawline. She remembered him being nice, if a bit shy and quiet.

"Polymir!" she called out again. Silence. She wondered whether she should venture inside the Kassel once she reached it.

He may have gone travelling, she reasoned. *That will be fun*, she thought unhappily, imagining having to try and find him all over his planet. She was still the size of her planet and walked through the woods back to the glass stairs, but then stopped herself. Where should she begin? The Kassel was still behind her. She closed her eyes to feel for his energy, but the chilly, brittle air made it difficult for her to focus.

She clenched her fist. She was just about to investigate the giant Kassel, when she heard a young man call out, "My, aren't you pretty!"

Navas froze. Who was *that*?

"Navas, dear, you shouldn't be here!" It was Polymir. The voices were calling from inside the Kassel, and she cocked her head. She couldn't see anyone through the windows as she reached the Kassel entrance.

"Polymir. I'm here to invite you to the Queen's birthday. I have a gift, too – it's from my sister, the Princess."

"Leave it on the steps—"

"Oh, let her in!" said the unknown voice jovially.

Navas wanted to know who Polymir was talking to. Maybe it was Crooked Dancer, or Entanerus?

"The Princess does not just give gifts," she called out. "She wants me to ensure everyone receives theirs in person."

She waited for a reply.

"I cannot see you, Navas," the voice was pleading.

"Polymir…" She wondered if he was post showered. "If you're… ermm… undressed, I understand, but just pop your head around the door so I can see you."

The younger voice laughed. "Can't we see her? I want to meet her. Let's get undressed anyway!"

There was a scuffle and, in front of Navas, the tall, black-painted door creaked open.

Just as Navas was about to enter, the door slammed shut on her.

"Fine! You're not invited to see the Queen!" Navas bent to leave the amethyst on the steps, when the curtain by the window beside the door flicked aside and then back again. "Oh, Polymir! This is silly, what's the matter?" Navas had her hands on her hips now. She looked up at the black Kassel, when the unknown voice spoke.

"My goodness, you are beautiful. Your breasts are full, your hair is so shiny, and your eyes are like pyres. And that flat stomach... I could eat a meal off of you!"

Navas wrapped her arms around herself. The visitor was watching her. She stepped away after depositing the amethyst on the steps. Walking away from the Kassel, she hid behind an old giant wheelbarrow and waited until Polymir, and guest, came out, which wasn't until after a long while. The door creaked open, and she gasped loudly. There wasn't another guest.

Polymir had two heads.

From the brief moment that she had seen him, she realised it was Polymir, but younger. They didn't hear her, and she had her hand clasped over her mouth. How could he have two heads? Did he *will* a companion to life? Was he sick? Navas wanted to take another look to make sure, but she quickly turned her head away in case she was caught. He had taken the amethyst, but he didn't want to be seen... Navas went back to the Kassel and spoke out loudly.

"Polymir... *Polymirs*... my sister and I look forward to seeing you... both. Please don't let the Princess down." Her voice was high and brittle.

She waited for a moment for a reply and Polymir the Younger called out happily, "We wouldn't miss this! I can't wait to see everyone!"

Navas nodded. "Th-thank you. I'll see you soon." She paused. "Are you OK? Really?" There was silence, then shuffling.

After a moment, a note slipped from under the large door with a little heart drawn in loose ink. Polymir loved to write.

Navas smiled as she held the large note and, as the ink was still wet, nimbly drew a heart with her fingertip and slid the note back under the door, over a bristly doormat. She waited a beat, but nothing. The black ink on her fingertip faded away in front of her eyes.

She took one more look at the Kassel, its beautiful shape pressed together by black peeling planks of wood and topped by sharp clay tiles. It took her a moment to realise her feet were being pierced by the mat, and so she left Polymir… Polymirs… to themselves.

Navas delved into the woods to find the glass bridge. Her neck felt so exposed, despite her heavy hair. The world around her kept shifting colours and the wind became colder. As she moved through the forest, she tripped over a branch. The soft, spongy sands began to settle around her. As she raised her head, she could see herself, for a fleeting moment, in the direction of the glass bridge, a version of her that looked distraught. As she tried to hoist herself up, she heard another rattle of cawing and she ran to the bridge, tripping up three times more.

She left Planet Polymir, her heart beating rapidly. She sat on the bridge top and panted, trying to process what she'd seen, the pain from the falls subsiding slowly. Heerajras felt pain but had a high threshold. Perhaps she should have stayed longer, but she was genuinely scared.
She felt sorry for Polymir. She hoped he… or them… would make it to the Queen's birthday party. Maybe he was lonely and had grown a friend. Could she grow a friend? Could anyone? She looked at her hands. She didn't even know where to start. She wriggled her fingers.

    From her vantage point, she could see the top of the planet clearly and watched as a storm span rigidly, forming a hexagon.
Despite this storm, which was a deep blue rather than a pale sandy colour, she'd seen no sign of it on the planet. She had no idea, whilst on the planet, that there was a storm.

Polymir and his planet were going through changes that she didn't understand. She wondered if Leifweiden could help him, or at least find out what was going on. She stood to dust herself off, yet not a grain of the planet's sand remained on her.

    Navas walked on and watched the sky for the red smudge as she did so. It was becoming cold; her nose began to go red, and her fingertips began to tingle. There were three amethysts left in her pouch.

Ahead of her was Planet Crooked Dancer, a gentle, mint-green gas planet that Navas had only passed, having never delved into the planet's softness.
She landed on a fluffy cloud that was dense enough to support her. Far off into the planet's horizon was a whole chain of these clouds, dipping beyond the horizon. Similar to Planet Polymir, it was quiet, and a light source shone in the sky that wasn't their Sun from this distance. The light source looked larger and dimmer than The Sun from her own planet, a chartreuse mist dampening its light.

Navas didn't have time to muse over the light for, as she took a step on the cloud to reach the next one, she suddenly became off-kilter. The whole horizon became vertical, and the floor became a wall. Navas thought she was falling but was still on her feet. The clouds scrolled down like giant raindrops and the soft light lit the clouds to a gentle yellow. However, unlike the sunsets at home, the light was pressed against the wall that should have been the planet's surface. The sky and horizon appeared to meet in the centre, like a reflection on the ocean back home, only the wrong way around.

From the ceiling of the world, Navas couldn't tell if this was the sky or the ground.

Despite her angle, a Kassel appeared slowly from the mint clouds in the distance the 'right' way up. It resembled a cluster of stalagmites, malachite in colour, but on the tips were red drips of liquid.

Navas had to steady herself. She clutched the pouch on her hip and called out to Crooked Dancer, trying to hide her panic.

As the clouds scudded vertically, she swallowed hard. Whatever angle she now was, her hair still remained swaying at her knee-backs, as if she was still upright. She felt it safer to hold the pouch in her fist.

She called and called and, finally, in the distance, she could hear chirps and squeaks.

Just as she was going to call out for Crooked Dancer again, he appeared upside down in front of her face, making her scream.

Navas fell backwards into the cloud. As she did so, the amethysts escaped from her pouch and fell down the side of the cloudy wall, disappearing into the softness.

She peered over, but suddenly felt dizzy and sat down where she was, hugging her knees.

Crooked Dancer had the appearance of a Heerajra, and his skin was the same soft green as his planet, his hair shaggy and emerald green. He looked like a teenager, slightly older than Princess Liras, but was so drawn and slim, he looked a lot older. His cheeks were hollow, and his large blue and red mismatched eyes were sunken. He wore tightly bound materials around his legs and a tight, blue, and yellow-striped vest with mini metal orange shoulder pads. His striped shorts were in contrasting purple, yellow and blue. Blue shaggy fur was tied around his elbows and knees, and he wore sandals made from thin, blue-coloured straw.

It was a lot to take in, even for the artist in Navas.

His movements were simian, and he made chirping noises without opening his mouth. He cocked his head when Navas stood up and, oddly, he reached into the 'sky' and retrieved the amethysts. He tossed them back to Navas, who thanked him profusely.

"Thank you, Crooked Dancer," she flustered. "We all would like you to come to the stars' birthday."

Crooked Dancer cocked his head again in misunderstanding and leapt down to meet Navas, completely stable, compared to Navas, who wished there was something she could grab hold to save her wobbling. She was feeling nauseous, watching the slow 'falling' clouds and being sideways as well. Crooked Dancer rolled out his long, pink tongue, spun it back up into his mouth and said in a squeaky voice, "ehca dna nrub rats eht ees ot emoc llahs I !ecin kool uoY !erofeb uoy nees reven evah I."

His blue eyes shone happily and Navas handed him an amethyst with a shaking hand. Oh, she hoped he understood her!

Crooked Dancer took the amethyst curiously and, within a beat, he ate the gem. Navas's jaw dropped.

"Oh, no that wasn't food!"

"derob gnitteg ma I,won evaeL .doog detsat tI."

Crooked Dancer stared back at Navas. They stared at each other for a few moments, interrupted only by the clouds trickling down the sky.

Navas made her thanks and had to find her way to the stairs on her own, heading back on herself. As she reached the first step, the entire planet corrected itself, in an awful jolt. Was this why the Queen didn't want her to visit the planet? Did Crooked Dancer consider the light in his sky his Majesty?

She pressed her temple and was on her knees when she reached the bridge.

"That planet…that boy…" She didn't want to get to her feet until the flipping in her stomach stopped. The Queen had never told her why the axis was not aligned, but she wondered if the planet had made the owner off-kilter – or was it the other way round?

Soon, the nausea subsided, and she caught sight of the wonderfully deep blue planet of Goston, the eighth planet from The Sun. It was a large planet and Navas was looking forward to seeing Goston herself, a young girl who was close to Princess Liras.

The Sun was smaller from here and she carried on, the blue of Planet Goston always making her yearn for her easel and paints.

Navas took a deep breath.

She reached Planet Goston and was immediately hit by the winds.

This planet was a constant storm.

The clouds were navy in colour and moved in large, heavy lurches. They resembled the churning ocean that took up most of the planet. Goston lived on a small island with a tall lighthouse and her Kassel was a boarding school. The many rooms were empty, except for her own.

Deepest blue waves smashed against the island and clouds bore lightning that pierced these waves.

Rain pelted down on Navas, and the glass steps were dangerously slick. Heavy metal chains ran down the length of the glassy steps and waves leapt up into the sky, as high and as sharp as mountains. It was so dark and blue. Lightning was the main light source here and it lit up the white foamy peaks of the waves. The light from the lighthouse washed over her and the boarding school, but it was dim compared to the flashing spears of light.

Although Navas had storms on her planet, they were a drizzle compared to the menacing, battering storms here. As Navas clung onto the chain, she slipped down the stairs and bounced to the salted, soaked shore, the salty white sand almost liquid from the thrashing rain and ocean.

The rain and winds made it hard to hear or see. Navas was sure the rain was darting sideways; such was the wind. She reached the boarding school and saw a few lights of the rooms turn off and on, and then one stayed on.

There was so much rain that standing upright was a task. As she drew closer to Goston's Kassel, she could see Goston peering from a window and then ducking away.

Within seconds, Goston was out in front of the building waiting for Navas. She was wearing a navy school pinafore over a white blouse, and black ribbons tied her denim blue hair into half-upside bunches. A red clip in her hair matched the red trim on her blouse and belt and the little bows on her white, knee-high socks. Her face was stricken, her charcoal eyes wide.
"Who are you?" she called as she grabbed Navas's waist. "What are you doing here? Is it bad that you're here? Oh, there is no one here to help me!" Goston was about twelve, panicked and in constant fear. Navas thought that this planet, with its menace and the weather, was not the calmest planet to be on. Maybe that was why Geadeous had to be strong-willed on her thunderous planet.
"Goston! Goston! It's me, Navas!"
Goston paced up and down and grabbed her head, gesticulating wildly.
"Navas? If you're here we must be doomed! Why is this happening?" In a swift second, Goston had gone back

inside her school building, and then in the ocean and then in front of Navas again, falling to her knees.

"Goston, here, take this," said Navas firmly. "This is for the Queen's birthday—" Goston shuddered and took the gleaming amethyst that Navas pressed into her drenched hand.

"Princess Liras... *oh* Princess Liras! This is all wrong!"

Goston wailed and screamed into the pale sand that made up the island and then, in another second, she was back by the lighthouse screaming. Goston would be still for a moment, then, in a blink, appear in a different spot. Navas couldn't keep up with how quickly Goston was moving. From the skyline, she saw a fork of lightning and the thunder boomed across the planet. There was so much rain. The heavy drops dragged Navas's hair down, and her clothes were weighed down from the water. She'd never complain about the rain back at home ever again.

Goston was gone, but her screams echoed against the wailing wind. Navas looked over at this ocean planet and wondered if, as on her planet, the waters ever calmed. Navas did hope that she could take some refuge in the boarding school, but reasoned Goston was in the best place to offer that.

She could see the lights of the boarding school switch on and off again as Goston raced between the rooms, and she wondered if she should stay for a while, despite being drenched. In the distance, she saw the black clouds twirl to a point and rain continued to bucket down on her. The wind's force was shocking. She was breathless and each part of her being was wet. Navas decided to leave; she'd lose herself otherwise.

The barrage of the storm was too much. She took another look at the boarding school and a harrowing cry came out of it. Even when she was younger, Goston was flighty and nervous. Navas wished she could take Goston away from here, but she didn't even know if the little girl would make it up the stairs. She hoped Goston was safe in her Kassel.

Navas climbed up the wet-slick steps of the bridge, trying to keep her balance in the wind. She spluttered and, as she reached the top of the stairs, she saw behind her a deep blue cloud begin to spiral in the distance as a waterspout was forming, a cylindrical tower of water that would certainly terrify poor Goston.

It connected to the ocean, and she didn't know whether to warn Goston, who was still flitting from room to room. A massive crack of thunder made her change her mind, as did the ever-approaching waterspout.

Navas reached the top of the glass bridge and was met by complete silence. She caught her breath and, from her vantage point, could see swirls of blues entwine from the surface of the ocean. Unlike Planet Polymir, the storm was visible from the bridge and within the world.

"Dearest Goston…" Navas thought she was so young and alone, but such was her homes conditions.

Navas wrung from her clothes as much water as she could, which splashed and froze on the bridge instantly. She was soddened. Her fingertips had crinkled just by being in the pelting rain. She was as dry as she could be, but the cold reached her instantaneously.

She needed to visit Planet Entanerus now before she froze. She assumed it was drier there. Sopping, cold and breathless, she continued in the now icy chill to the last planet of their solar system.

Princess Liras, back on The Moon, was continuing her practice on the veena and took a moment to ponder. She wondered how Navas was doing and rested the instrument vertically, so that she could rest her cheek against the bridge. Liras closed her eyes and hoped her sister would be back soon. She lay the instrument down and decided she wanted a 'lie-on-the-grass-in-the-Sun' break.

Planet Entanerus was the smallest planet in the solar system. It was close to the size of The Moon, but not as beautiful. There wasn't a long staircase to reach the planet; instead, it was nothing more than a curb from the glass bridge. Navas shrank to the size she would be on her own planet, and realised there wasn't room for a Kassel here.

After a short distance, she found Entanerus sitting on an intricately carved wooden throne, in a white, silk hanfu that flowed down to the base of the throne. He wore a white mian guan, with a small crown upon his head, with nitrogen pearls that hung from either side of the square headdress. The detailing on his clothes meandered into patterns of whorls as found on trees. Entanerus was young, aged about eight, and appeared to be carved out of wood, similar to a puppet. He even had a hinged jaw, but he didn't open his mouth.

It was cold on his planet and Navas's breath came out in plumes. Her clothes were freezing over slightly, as she was still damp from the deluge from Planet Goston. She shivered and wrapped her arms around herself. She towered over Entanerus, but she didn't want to crouch near him so as not to talk to him as if he were a child… She couldn't see his legs at all…
"Entanerus, I've come to invite you to see the Queen. It's her birthday soon."

Navas handed him an amethyst, but he still didn't move. His only movement was from his little chest as it moved in and out, his breath visible.
She placed the amethyst on the armrest and Entanerus's eyes locked onto it. Even his irises looked like pale wood that was varnished so that they caught the light.

It seemed to be night on this planet, but there was also some light that reached here. Above her, Navas could see the stars like she could back at home, but they seemed flatter here, as if they were painted on a dome ceiling, and had no depth.
Navas smiled slightly. She crouched in front of Entanerus. She'd never seen him before. He was beautiful to look at. She followed his gaze as he looked out of his planet, and gasped.

She could see the darkest space above her, but either side of her were replicated images of herself, as if mirrors had been placed in front of each other. Becoming disorientated, Navas panicked, unable to see how she could get off the planet. Looking up, the stars were now lamps, larger spotlights that shone their light over the pair. It all resembled a diorama of the very real planet she was on.

She took a step back and the mirror images blurred until she saw the glass step.
She then wondered if Entanerus was looking at himself constantly in the mirrors. Her face became sympathetic. What did he see if he had lived here forever? Maybe he

didn't even know who the Queen was? Navas looked back down at him, and he was still looking at the amethyst, his arm unmoved. Remaining still, she tried to visually delve into the infinite image.

She saw herself, again and again, falling into the darkness. She felt trapped but it was curiously addictive to see how far her image went.
As Navas stared, she tilted her head and it took Entanerus to move his eyes, just a slight noise of friction, to remind herself to snap out of it. She turned and smiled at him. The planet and sky returned, as if the mirrors were a trick of her mind.
It was so quiet here. There was no storm or wind to disrupt *his* mind.
"Please do come, we're all wanting to see you," said Navas. Her voice was a little shaken.

She left Entanerus and from the glass bridge, looked out into the expanse of space. His was such a small planet, with no room for a Kassel or sky. It felt good to have an unconfined view.

Now, she had to make her way back home. Navas rested on the bridge for a moment and closed her eyes. Her damp clothes were making her colder, and she had a fleeting thought to retrieve the blanket from Leifweiden. She wanted the blanket to embrace her. *But he is so busy*, she thought hazily.

Looking back, there were no other Heerajras to visit. No more moons, no more neighbours. Just the endless breadth of space. This was her family, and she wanted them to be together as much as Princess Liras did. She stood and began to walk back home. She passed Planet Goston and hoped that Goston would see a calm, sunny day one day. Even if it was on her own planet with her sister. She passed Planet Geadeous and Planet Polymir, the Heerajra elders of her family, and wondered if they would make it to the gathering. Crooked Dancer, she assumed, would turn up if they had understood each other.

She passed Planet Leifweiden and looked up at the spot where he thought the red smear was. Navas couldn't see anything and was thankful that he was looking out for them. She wanted to jump down and see him, but she figured he was preoccupied, and she was eager to see her sister. She blew him a kiss and looked forward to seeing him again when he was more relaxed and skipped back home.

Navas made it home and immediately flopped onto the grass and took a deep breath. The Sun was out, and it was warm, such a welcome change from the coldness of the outside world.

She wanted a cup of tea and was surprised to see Princess Liras sitting in the studio, tea ready.

"How did you know I'd be here?" asked Navas.

Princess Liras hugged her sister and gave her a mug. "I didn't, I just kept popping down. Don't tell Her Majesty."

"Oh, well, I have to now."

Princess Liras wasn't listening and looked distracted. "So," her bejewelled hands began to flap, "so, you are back. How was it, sister? Please don't give me bad news."

Princess Liras looked very nervous. Navas smiled sadly.

"I'd sit down, if I were you." Princess Liras drew in a breath but didn't sit down.

"They... were thankful, but no one is coming, sister. They can't make it."

Liras nodded quickly, her eyes welling up. She avoided looking at her sister. "Oh... that's... a shame." As she spoke, Navas had turned her head and was trying to suppress her laughter. Princess Liras gasped on noticing her and exclaimed, "You're a mean person!" Princess Liras clenched her fists and left the studio. A laughing Navas followed her and hugged her from behind.

"They're all coming, sister. Everyone."

Princess Liras sniffed. "You're mean."

Navas hugged her harder. "I'll take that as a thank you." Soon, Princess Liras was smiling, but began crying as she had started the process.

"Her Majesty will be so happy. Thank you, sister. How was everyone?" she sniffed.

They sat down on the sun-washed grass and Navas relished the warmth for a moment. "We'll need another tea," she replied. "Where do I start?"

Navas then proceeded to tell Princess Liras about everyone, their planets and the Heerajras themselves. Princess Liras couldn't contain her happiness. She was slightly worried about Geadeous but, overall, the Queen would be so happy to see everyone together at the same time.

She owed this all to her sister.

Princess Liras had met everyone when she was very young, while in the arms of the Queen. Like a proud mother, the Queen had taken her to meet the rest of the Heerajras on the glass bridge connections. Princess Liras vaguely remembered the different colours and energies but couldn't recall all the faces to match them with the planets. Except for Iros and Goston, but it was a long time ago.

There was a time before the Heerajras were due to meet up.

Iros was back at home from Planet Geadeous, and she lay on her couch, holding the amethyst up to a light beam. She could stare at it forever. She sat up and looked at all of her wonderful drinks. She'd make a special drink for the Queen and wanted it to be as bright yellow as she could.

Moreover, she wanted the drink to get the Queen as drunk as possible. She was looking forward to seeing everyone and, subtly, she wondered what drama Geadeous wanted to cause.

She loved Geadeous's attitude. Be the best person you could, regardless of what people may say. It wasn't right to disrespect the Queen, but Geadeous was respecting herself. Iros smiled hazily, the purple light of the gem bouncing off of her hand. The meeting meant so much to Princess Liras. Iros decided *some* drama was ok.

Celd Dion was winding down on his planet and sat on an upturned watering can. He was watching his yellow clouds roll by, cigar in one hand and amethyst in the other.

He scratched his neck. Maybe he should materialise lighter clothes, but he never wanted to not look smart. You never knew who would visit – although, he could have done without seeing that unkempt girl. His black corn swayed gently, and he wanted to pick the best for his Queen. Was that being eager? *No*, he thought. The Queen should know he is there for her, and how much he values her. Celd Dion had met her once, and it was enough to measure all other women against her.

He remembered when he was younger, as young as the Princess, seeing a beckoning light that shone through his heavy, shielding clouds. As he climbed the stairs from out of his planet, he saw a beautifully radiant woman standing before him, wearing white robes, the colours of the rainbow rushing through them. He remembered her hand outstretched and so much light, that rippled and glimmered. He could never forget her gentle smile, a genuine, pleased-to-see-you smile.
He lit another cigar after stubbing out his used one and, very slowly, took off his tweed jacket. The woman embodied class, intelligence and elegance. Their meeting on the glass bridge was all too brief.
Then he recalled when Navas came bumbling down to his home for the first time, hair pulled in every direction, her skirt waving like a flag as she bounded over his crops. She was probably the same age then as the

Princess was now, but their mindsets couldn't have been more separate. He still didn't believe the two were of kin. The air became hotter. He closed his eyes and breathed deeply. The Queen would feast on his corn and his black waters. He would show everyone he was the one whom she favoured.

Geadeous was materialising different robes in front of a giant mirror and admiring her wonderful reflection. She placed the gifted amethyst on her chest and wondered if she could fashion a necklace out of it. Poor Navas, wanting to be met with cheer when she invited her to see the Queen.
Geadeous looked at the painting that depicted her as a virago.
She thought back to when, in the solar system, it was just her and Glaruntia.
  The planets were sore, red and combining slowly. Her tyrant form had come from this. It was the only way she could survive the turmoil and chaos around them. Geadeous remembered she was about eight when she first knew she could become a tyrant. It frightened her,

her change into another being. Flames and lava fell about her and there were collisions of rocks and matter and light... but, in this disruption, Glaruntia frolicked.

The Queen was both genders and neither gender, and had a dual-gendered voice. As much as she could pass off looking like a Heerajra, and was classed under this canopy, beings made from stars were made of a different energy to the other Heerajras as they were not born from planets.

When she was younger, Glaruntia looked more like a young boy. The boy version of her had short, golden hair, and wore a white tunic, with gold trim, and sandals that left bursts of rainbow where his foot connected to space. He was about fifteen and resembled a fairy, Geadeous remembered. He would flit from one angered planet to the next, finding the noise and drama incredibly fun and exciting. This was before the glass bridges, so Geadeous had to watch from debris, this carefree fairy not giving a single damn about her. He knew she was there, because he'd wave to her as he flew and flitted. How could he be so carefree and excited by the mess and anger around him?

Geadeous had never told anyone about this.

It was a memory that she kept a secret, as none of the others had been there. They were born after her planet was born.

Once the planets had settled into their new existence, the others never knew the disorder that came before them. And anyway, Geadeous knew that no one would believe that their Queen had once been an unheeding goblin.

When Geadeous became a virago, her golden armour materialising over her small frame, Glaruntia was thankful, honoured. Geadeous was glad to have protected the others from harm. Their world was born from agony and pain, and she didn't want the others to witness what she had. Geadeous had become powerful, able to protect herself with armour and sword, and had become a being capable of catapulting meteorites away from their homes. Yet, it still wasn't enough. A loud crack of thunder lit up her world and rumbled for the longest time afterwards.

Geadeous went over to the window and realised her planet was still in turmoil.

Would it be best not to even go? She placed a hand on the pane of glass and vowed to protect her world and her feelings.

Polymir was in his sombre Kassel, quill in hand and a blank sheet of paper in front of him, the amethyst sparkling next to his inkwell.
The Younger was talking incessantly, and Polymir the Elder was noticing he was losing more and more control of his left side. His left hand was gesticulating more than he had ever seen it before.
"Please do say we can go," pestered the Younger. "If not, I can go by myself, can I not?"
The Elder resisted crying. He wanted silence; he wanted to think and reflect. He had tried to befriend this head, hate it, hurt it, but it was him, another part of him he had never known. What in the world had Navas thought when seeing him? That sweet, foolsome child.
He looked at the blank sheet of paper. He wanted to write a poem for his Queen but couldn't think for a second. Oh, how he wanted to be in her protective light.
"Can I have a moment? To write to the Queen, please?"

The Younger grinned. "So, we *are* going! What are we going to wear? What are you writing? Can I write? Let's write a letter together!"

Polymir the Elder smiled emptily. The Younger wouldn't stop talking. Polymir the Elder felt his heart ache. The Elder quickly put out of his mind the thought of deafening himself just so he didn't have to hear the Younger's chatter.

He looked out the window and out over the stark woods and tried to remember his living world before. It was peaceful and gave him time to write, to conceive, and it inspired his writings. He felt a tremble of nerves in his stomach and the Younger waved his own hand dismissively.

"By then... I should be free of you, perhaps. I can then meet this Queen on my own, old man."

The Elder nodded slowly, and his quill-filled hand began to shake. He wondered if the Queen's rays would help his world flourish again. Her kindness and energy, and her ever calm being.

"Perhaps," he replied. "Perhaps we shall be two by then. But, until then, please may I have peace?"

The Younger laughed. "Oh, why? Peace is so boring! And wouldn't it be easier to cut my tongue off?"

Crooked Dancer was busy placing the amethyst in a cave, a frosted frigid alcove of diamonds, rubies and Heerajra skulls of varying sizes. He crept in and placed the gem carefully in the centre of his treasure, as the skulls, rubies and precious stones clattered and sparkled. Patting the amethyst gently, he floated up and out the cave and rested on a cloud that was horizontal to him, but vertical in movement, arms behind his back and legs crossed.

He was happy seeing the pretty lady from wherever she was from. *Maybe she could get me more lovely jewels*, he thought. He turned his head to view his Kassel, almost hand moulded with its bumps and unclean sides. *Maybe next time I'll invite her in.* His face pulled into a slothful smile. His entire Kassel was inverted, with furniture and floors on ceilings and candle chandeliers upright from the floors. Stairs led to false doors and windows led to new rooms. Crooked Dancer found humour in imagining Navas getting lost in his chilled, capsized Kassel. He closed his eyes and nestled into the cloud.

Whatever he had to do, he had time.

Goston was under her bed, cowering from the storm outside. Photos of massive, black-sailed ships rattled on the walls and the wood creaked and grinded in the room, as the storm raged on. She wished she could be braver. She wished she could go outside, but she was scared. It was terrifying, the darkness and noise. Under her bed, shaking, she gripped the amethyst, thinking of Princess Liras. She was so pretty and kind. Goston wanted to be just like her when she got older. She remembered Princess Liras visiting her when she was about ten and Princess Liras telling her she was very brave to be here. Goston had never seen the outside world and had never stepped off her sodden planet. As much as her storms were brutal, she'd always assumed there were worse storms outside of her planet. Only through a break in the cumbersome clouds had she seen a single star.

Goston closed her eyes and screamed when a crack of lightning exploded above her.

"I'm not brave," she wailed. She curled up in a ball, quivering, the amethyst safe in her pale, screwed-up hand.

Entanerus barely moved as a quiet wind passed him in his chair. He slid his eyes to see the amethyst, subtly sparkling on his arm rest.

He remembered the Queen, a long time ago was her visit. His memory recalled white robes and light.

With his left hand, he pressed a small button on the armrest and four mechanical legs popped out from under his chair, jointed and long, like spider legs. The frost snapped around his chair base as the legs pumped slightly to get ready for movement.

He had such a long way to walk, he wanted to start his journey now.

Leifweiden was looking up at the stars and staring intently at the red smudge. As he moved, he knocked the amethyst over. He had taken it up with him to his watchtower. He smiled. He was looking forward to seeing everyone and thought of Navas sitting on his lap. He wished she didn't have to leave so suddenly.

Although they didn't spend *enough* time together, he knew she had to look after Princess Liras, and it endeared Navas to him.

Leifweiden had to look after everyone.

He viewed the quiet volcano through his telescope and knew this would be the key to their protection. He didn't trust the tarnish in the sky.

He resisted viewing Navas through his telescope and, instead, took a break. He visited the volcano and, when he arrived at the base, said to it, "Please be dead. I don't want you to wake up again." When he was younger, his pre-ice world was hot and volcanic, then black from the dried lava, and eventually cool enough to welcome snow.

Leifweiden much preferred the snow. His home was muted, to allow him to wonder about the skies above him.

He climbed to the top of the volcano and sighed. When the observatory was complete, he'd invite Navas here so they could both view this world together. He'd brought his telescope with him and checked one last time for the red smear through the eyepiece.

It'd gone.

After scanning the skies, his panic soon brought relief. *Maybe it had been just a fleeting mark in the sky?* he thought, trying his best to be rational. He collapsed his telescope as he sat on the crater edge, not realising how hard he was gripping the telescope in his hand. "Just be fleeting," he whispered. Without his telescope, he watched the far stars and the gentle light from outlying galaxies. Before long, snow lay heavily on his shoulders and hair.

Navas was in her Kassel and had sketched out all the Heerajras as if they were posing in front of a camera. She and Liras were in front, grinning from ear to ear. She wanted to give this hurried sketch to the Queen, but wondered if she should give her a painting instead... She slid the sketch under her bed, smudging it slightly. She wouldn't forget it was there, she reasoned.

She lay on the bed and stared out at the night sky, soft gentle stars ebbing their lights out to her. She sighed happily and turned to sleep; her thoughts filled with what she had seen on her journey.

The Dinner

On the dawn of the gathering, some twenty Planet Navas years after Navas sent out the invites personally to her family, Princess Liras went to visit the Queen. She was still in her purple lengha and bright silver jewels. Just as she was about to step out onto the glass bridge, she changed her mind and went to grab her sister.

      She found Navas after a while, sitting on a mountain top, a small easel in one hand and charcoal in the other. Navas was working on a sketch, battling the slight flurry of snow.

Princess Liras had to climb up the mountain, as the only Heerajra that could float on his planet was Crooked Dancer. She narrowed her eyes against the wind.

"I don't want to meet you here when it's urgent. Can you come with me? To see the Queen."

Navas took a moment to answer her sister. "It's early, no?"

Princess Liras smiled and sat down with her sister, brushing off the snow as it landed on her. "I want you to come with me. I couldn't have done this without you."

"Ah, but you could have, sister." Navas gathered her art supplies and, with her free hand, held her sister's hand. "Do you think I'll be able to finish my sketch off?"

"You can! Afterwards."

Navas smiled doubtfully.

"Let's go, Lili. I'll lose you under the snow in no time!"

Liras resisted. "Wait, we must get you dressed up! It will be fun!" She clasped her hands together. "I'm thinking of a full Anarkali in green and blue…"

Navas screwed up her nose. "I'll think about it. I'll take some earth with me so I can change."

She began her climb down the mountain and Princess Liras sighed. *No, you won't*, she thought.

***

Navas hadn't seen The Sun so close up in a long time. It wasn't just the obvious heat that was apparent. The energy felt was immense. Navas felt a long, prickly sensation in her whole body as a result of being so close to the burning orb. The Sun was mainly orange, but had fantastic whorls of deep amber and red, with pockets of black that were quickly washed away with lighter yellows.

Loops of plasma sprung from the surface and back into the fiery waters. They seemed as if they were going to shoot off The Sun, like giant arches of hot honey, but fell back down, never to be seen again. To Navas, the falling plasma sounded like rainfall as it fell back down.

There was so much energy here and Princess Liras knew The Sun had softened her energy, just in case she or the other Heerajras wanted to visit. The Queen, until this point, had only allowed Princess Liras and Iros into the palace, and had met the Heerajras on the glass bridge near their planets.

It was so big, too. Planets like Planet Geadeous were titanic enough, but compared to The Sun? Planet Navas was the size of a pebble compared to their star. But it was fantastic to look at. The yellow disc from Planet Navas now became this mutating, unstill sphere that never relented with its changing colour gradient. Closer still, the liquid gas became a shimmery gold, the larger pockets of falling gas becoming cooler and hotter. The colour and flames levelled out into a wonderful molten mess of dark and light gold, thickly covering the sphere.

Navas and Princess Liras followed the bridge until they saw the Queen's home. The bridge didn't end on a pole of The Sun, so the Heerajras would have to float the rest of the way to reach the Kassel, which was the size of a city. There were so many rooms and skyscrapers, separated by roads, that the owner had free rein to live in any of the hundreds of thousands of rooms available to her. The Queen herself mainly stayed in her palace, where all her roads and pavements led to, surrounded by fountains of fire and orange plasma.

    Her home, including the city, was made entirely of gold. The palace went out for miles on either side and there were millions of windows cast in black glass. It was perfectly symmetrical, and other than the fountains, there were seven huge gold statues of Heerajras. Navas didn't recognise them, and, from her angle, they were difficult to view fully, but they wore robes and carried harps and bridles all in gold.

The air was torrid on The Sun, sparkling with gold glitter. Everything sang with heat and shone like white light on a calm ocean.

Navas exhaled.

Princess Liras smiled. "I know. None of us can stay here for long, but imagine this at full energy?" She walked on ahead to the great gold doors of the palace that were studded with yellow diamonds, and they opened automatically to allow the sisters in.

Inside, the palace was mostly in baroque design, and it was all gold, as if carved from a mountainous gold ore. Navas touched her cleavage where she had hidden her sketch and wondered when she should give this to the Queen. She had a small rock that she had taken from her home hidden in her cleavage, together with the sketch of the Heerajras.

The sisters faced an imperial staircase and Navas had to admit that this was far more glamorous than Geadeous's mansion.

"It's so pretty."

"It is," agreed Liras. "The Queen stays in the palace so that we can visit. But she becomes her true size when she's on her own. Can you stay here? I need to see the Queen. I won't be too long, don't get bored."

Navas nodded, still in awe of just how glorious it all was here, as she sat on a stair step. The framed paintings on the walls moved, living photos of galaxies and stars. The ceiling 'painting' was the entire solar system, complete with glass bridge and large stars drawn with five points. Navas noted that this wasn't a particularly well-reflected painting. However, she was more than entertained as she stared at these painted videos.

Princess Liras met the Queen, who was seated in the throne room. She wore mostly white, a white cassock, a chasuble with the seven colours of the rainbow on the interior, and a mitre, the colours of the rainbow at its forefront. Gold ran through the sash she wore. She held a gold sceptre, with a diamond on top. She also wore a smaller gold cape around her shoulders, and her ever so long cape, gossamer thin, faded off from her shoulders if she was indoors. Outside, she'd allow it to be free, as gold as her own sun rays.

Her soft, wavy hair, which was ash blonde in colour, fell just to her shoulders and she had very pale white skin that shimmered. There was nothing to claim the gender of this Heerajra and, when this Heerajra spoke, both male and female voices were heard.

"My dear Princess, how are you?"

Princess Liras curtsied and said happily, "I have a gift for you. All of your children are visiting today. For your birthday." Princess Liras looked so flushed and happy that the Queen didn't have the heart to tell her she had known about this already. Stars energies were so strong that they could use their entire body and beings to see out into the solar system, and sometimes beyond.

Stars couldn't hear that far but could see out as far as their energies could reach, when they were in a focused state.

"Come, and receive my thanks, dear Princess," requested the Queen. Princess Liras knelt and kissed the Queen's left hand, dodging the woven gold rings. "I cannot wait to see everyone. Let's wait here until they arrive." Princess Liras nodded and sat on the floor like a little girl, unable to contain her happiness and excitement. She looked up at the Queen and saw a subtle gleam emanate from her.

Navas was nervous. She didn't know who would be arriving for the gathering and closed her eyes. She could hear the fires of The Sun, with the sounds of metallic ringing and a constant hum.
The plasma falling up and down sounded so much like rain and Navas realised it didn't sound too dissimilar to a water-soaked day. For such a fiery world, it had so many sounds resembling water.

  As she waited in the grand entrance, Celd Dion, who hadn't aged one minute, arrived. He walked in, looked up at the palace's high ceilings and then stood furthest away from Navas. He held the ears of his black corn, and a bottle of his oil, in a black woven basket. Navas observed him trying not to gawp at the immense size of the palace. Luckily, the tall, redwood doors remained open for guests. Navas didn't think any of the Heerajras could swing even the knocker, even Geadeous. As the two waited, Entanerus arrived, his eyes unmoving. Navas was astonished to see his throne had four mechanical legs. From his cold world, even on Planet Navas he would have been too hot, Navas thought in wonder.

The spidery vehicle parked up and Navas and Celd Dion stared. Navas wondered if Celd Dion had ever met Entanerus. She thought he would say hello, but alas Entanerus was a child and Celd Dion ignored him. Navas waved to Entanerus, who remained motionless.
Happily, Leifweiden and Iros arrived. He hugged Navas, then shook Celd Dion's hand and knelt to say hello to Entanerus.
There was no reply from Entanerus, so Leifweiden chatted to Celd Dion and Iros smiled at Navas.
"Where's the Princess?" Leifweiden asked.
"With the Queen." Navas smiled contentedly at Leifweiden. The awkwardness of their last visit was gratefully forgotten.
"Oh, you'll have all day with him. Chat to me," directed Iros. "Isn't this place fancy?"
Navas nodded to Iros. "She could house all of us here."

Iros took a bottle out of a black leather bag she carried with her. It was a gold-coloured, sparkling drink in a tall bottle. "Think we can have some before we go in?"
"Iros, put that away," Leifweiden smiled.
"It won't last too long! Aren't you nervous?"
He shook his head and looked around him. "She's here for us, isn't she?" He tugged at his scarf slightly. *This heat*, he thought agitatedly.
Iros went over to Leifweiden and Navas followed. "I'm sure this place is getting bigger and bigger. How are you, Celd Dion?" Iros asked, so politely that she knew it would irritate him. She smiled at him in his discomfort.
"Why do you ask, child?" barked Celd Dion.
Iros grinned. "You're such a grump!" She folded her arms as she said this. Celd Dion looked down at her and, just as he was about to say something, she turned to Entanerus.
She got up very close to him, admiring and studying him as if he was in a museum display.

Navas realised that all the Heerajras were technically their own heights on their own planet. However, in a room, they were all relative, give or take a foot or so. Iros didn't tower over Celd Dion, and Celd Dion *looked* older than Entanerus, so was naturally taller and bigger than the child. There was room for all the Heerajras to reach planet size and still fit comfortably in the palace; yet, in this hall, everything was to scale. It wasn't often a Heerajra, or the Queen, would need to be as large as their celestial home unless they were travelling on the bridge.

Leifweiden and Navas both smiled at each other, and he couldn't resist taking her hands. "Are you well?" he asked. Navas saw the red on his sleeves that was reaching up to his elbows. The red didn't match anything he was wearing.

She nodded and blushed slightly. They could both feel Celd Dion glaring, so Leifweiden squeezed her hand and said he'd talk to her later. Navas went to join Iros and, as she did so, Goston entered the palace in tears. She halted when she stepped into the main hall and wailed even harder. Navas ran over to her, Celd Dion rolling his eyes. Navas knelt in front of the young girl and hugged her hard, wiping her tears away.

"You made it, darling. It's ok, we're here now."

"It was so scary!" Goston wept.

Iros hung back, not sure what to say. "So, you're Goston? I'm Iros. If you stop crying, you can have some of this drink. It's for the Queen, but you're just as special, right?"

Goston sniffed loudly and began to shake. "I wanna go home!"

Iros patted her head. "The Queen wants to see you." Iros shook the bottle so that the gold glitter rushed inside. "This will help."

Navas smiled as Goston shook like a frail leaf. "Thank you, Iros."

"Not even lying," said Iros. "The Queen said she'd not seen Goston in a while."

"When was the last time you were here?" Navas asked.

"The palace?" asked Iros. "Don't remember. The bar the Queen has? A few years back. You should see it… the bar literally has no end."

She looked at the bottle in her hands and sat on the steps with Goston. "We'll have a few sips, ok?" Navas was surprised to see Iros looking out for Goston. How brave Goston was to come here all by herself.

Just as Iros had calmed Goston down slightly, Polymir walked in, wearing a white silk sheet over the second face.

There was silence when he walked in.

"Polymir?" Leifweiden asked quietly.

"Leifweiden, Celd Dion, it's a pleasure. Ladies. Children?" The Elder tilted his head slightly when he saw Entanerus.

He stood away from everyone, but they all saw the white sheet moving slightly as the younger Polymir inhaled and exhaled.

Leifweiden smiled brightly at him and carried on talking to Celd Dion, who did his best not to stare. Leifweiden and Celd Dion had met a few times, had been to each other's planets, and got on, despite Celd Dion's crankiness.

Iros and Goston couldn't stop staring at Polymir, and Iros involuntarily gripped Goston's hand too hard when Polymir the Younger moved his head side to side under the sheet, as if to alleviate a stiffness. Navas placed her finger over her lips as Iros mouthed, *"What is that?"*

Navas didn't answer her. Polymir had made the tough decision to arrive. She tried to gesture to Iros that she would 'tell her later', but Iros, who couldn't understand the jumpy hand signals, rolled her eyes dismissably. Iros sipped more from the bottle and kept offering some to Goston, who was staring at the floor, not wanting to look at the scary man in the corner.

Crooked Dancer bounded in and danced up the stairs and then back down again. He was happiest floating and so they all watched him reach the landing banister, where he sat, looking down at everyone, rocking his legs out. Navas waved to him, and his long tongue rolled out like a scroll again.

Goston looked close to fainting.

Crooked Dancer was in his own little world and so carefree. Polymir the Elder sighed slightly.

"Who is that?" Celd Dion asked Leifweiden.

"Crooked Dancer, I think. He seems happy, doesn't he?"

"Very... improper." Celd Dion glared and Crooked Dancer didn't notice at all.

Navas smiled. *Oddly, he can float constantly*, she thought in bemusement.

Princess Liras walked out through the landing doors that met the two staircases. She was surprised to see Crooked Dancer, who spun around and then waved at her.

"Oh, hello! My dear family," she said regally to everyone else. "The Queen is ready to see us all."

Just as she turned, Geadeous arrived, her steps heavy as she couldn't dramatically throw the doors open. Their eyes locked on to each other's.

"Princess Liras," Geadeous bowed. The room became silent again.

Princess Liras inhaled sharply. "Geadeous. You're in time for dinner. Please, this way."

Princess Liras led them all to the main dining hall. Iros whispered to Geadeous, "You're a little late!"

"And you're a little drunk."

"I needed it, I was nervous," Iros giggled.

"It's not you who should be nervous."

As Princess Liras took her seat at the dining table, she breathed out quickly. She wanted to perform her music after dinner and hoped the dinner would be a success.

She felt nervous, but excited too. Not just about the dinner, but her performance for the Queen. No matter what happened, she thought determinedly, her song would bring peace.

The Queen sat at the head of the table, and everyone had to bow to her before they entered the dining room. Geadeous remained standing tall.
It had seemed the Queen had met everyone, but not necessarily on their planets, Navas mused.

It seemed the further out the planet was, the less anyone had seen of them. She'd only met some of the Heerajras once, like Polymir. Navas tried to think back to when they would have all met. Liras and The Sun had met everyone. She herself had previously visited everyone bar Crooked Dancer, Entanerus and Geadeous, although she had met Geadeous on her bridge. Leifweiden and Celd Dion had visited each other, and she couldn't forget the time, as 'teenagers', Leifweiden had been to her home planet.

It seemed the outer Heerajras hadn't stepped off of their own planets before, except perhaps when Geadeous went to visit Iros.
This is why the birthday is important to Liras, she realised.
Navas was sitting between Crooked Dancer and Goston, who was seated next to Polymir, the white sheet still over the Younger's face.
Glaruntia sat between Princess Liras and Iros. Iros sat next to Celd Dion, who was next to Leifweiden, and he was beside an empty chair. Geadeous was seated opposite Glaruntia. Entanerus, who sat next to Geadeous, was raised in his seat, having no legs to sit on a chair.

The dining room was huge. Through the thin, tall windows, the blazing Sun could be seen outside, a haze of light and glitter. Black moonstone chandeliers hung from the ceiling. The table was laid out exquisitely. Everything was so marvellous, Navas felt that she was out of her depth here. There were several forks and knives laid out from the plates. There were several plates. There were vases on the table filled with slivers of fanned-out metals and candles tipped with little white flames. She looked over at Princess Liras, who smiled. Her sister looked at home. Navas wondered if she should have worn something nicer, maybe even changed her hairstyle, but then realised that no one else had changed, either. There was charcoal under her nails. She pressed on the little hidden rock she held in her top. The next time Princess Liras wanted her to dress up, she would, she decided. Even if it was for a day… or an evening. Navas quickly glanced at the beautiful Geadeous, who was trying to hide her awe as everything was so wonderful.

The Queen addressed everyone when they were all seated, and she raised a glass of red plasma. Everyone followed suit, bar Crooked Dancer, who was mesmerised by the sheen of one of his knives.

"My family, I thank you so much for being here. Thank you, Princess Liras, for arranging this gathering."

Princess Liras smiled. "It was thanks to my sister. I couldn't have done this without her."

Navas went dark green and could feel everyone looking at her.

"Then I must thank your sister. Let's eat."

The Queen moved her hand and plasma food appeared on their plates. Although it was plasma, there were solid foods, as well as liquid items, but it was all coloured a milky purple, strewn with baby-blue bands of colour. The Queen looked at Navas.

"It must have been a long journey. You had to visit everyone. I do hope everyone welcomed you kindly?"

Navas nodded and hoped Celd Dion felt bad. Before she could reply, Polymir the Younger spoke up from under his sheet.

"I wished I could have met her properly. She's so pretty."

Everyone stopped eating and stared at Polymir. Goston whimpered. Leifweiden looked decidedly tight jawed. The Queen's eyes were large, and Polymir the Elder stared at his food, hoping no one had heard the Younger speak.

"Polymir. Can you explain the mask?" the Queen asked carefully.

She could see Polymir the Younger breathing under the sheet. Princess Liras noticed Goston going whiter and whiter. Iros stared at him, eyes wide and eager to see what was under his sheet.

"Your Majesty, it's nothing—" However, before Polymir the Elder could finish, the Younger whipped off the sheet, prompting Goston, Iros and Princess Liras to scream.

Goston was so scared she ended up sitting on Navas's lap and buried her face into her chest, the sketch rustling as it was being pressed into.

As Navas held Goston, Iros still couldn't stop screaming until Celd Dion had to place his hand on hers. He was shocked still, and Leifweiden and Geadeous both looked on, their mouths open in shock.

The Queen's eyes were as wide as saucers. As everyone stared, Crooked Dancer chirped and said, "!won owt sah eH !ecaf sih ta kooL."

Entanerus had moved his eyes but hadn't seen enough to consider it abnormal to see a Heerajra with two heads.

"Polymir?" The Queen tried to gather her thoughts and said quickly, "Goston, that is enough, child."

Goston buried her face in Navas's chest.

"What's wrong with you? Why do you have two heads?" Iros exclaimed. Geadeous almost laughed out loud at Iros's boldness.

Celd Dion retracted his hand from that of Iros, but he kept his arm behind her back, stunned into silence. Princess Liras already knew from Navas's accounts that Polymir had two heads but seeing it in real life was a different matter. She tried to not breathe so erratically.

Elder Polymir looked like he was going to cry. "My Majesty, I cannot say, it happened so slowly. I feel like he is going to break away from me one day." He stood up to leave, knocking over his heavy chair.

The Queen looked to the Younger and asked, "Can you understand me?"

Princess Liras had never seen the Queen this pale before.

The Younger grinned. "You? Of course I can. This old man never told me you were so beautiful. Everyone is, aren't they?"

Iros tried to look affronted on behalf of the Queen, but a smile fluttered on her lips. Celd Dion decided she didn't need comforting any longer. This wasn't a laughing matter in his opinion.

"Yes. We all are. Polymir—" The Queen was inching her words out.

"He is called the Elder and I am the Younger." The Younger turned to his older face. "I will be you one day, won't I?" The Younger saw the Queen pull a concerned face.

"Don't worry, Your Majesty. I won't hurt him. I'll be glad to be free of this old man."

The Queen nodded slowly. She wanted to make sure they were both ok. "It'll be fine," she said lightly. "You're with your family now."

"Why didn't you ask for help?" Geadeous asked.

"I was frightened," the Elder said. "It was a child's head, to begin with…"

"I need a drink." Iros plonked her bottle of gold liquid onto the table. Goston was still quivering, and Navas asked if she wanted to sit next to Leifweiden. Goston began to cry.

Princess Liras said to her, "Goston, my sister cannot eat with you on her lap. Polymir won't hurt you."

Goston sniffed loudly. "Sorry, Navas."

Iros poured the gold liquid out for Goston, who drank it in one, her two trembling hands holding the goblet tightly.

Navas slowly manoeuvred Goston to her own chair. "It's alright, Goston."

The Younger Polymir looked to Goston and said, "If you scream again, I'll eat you." Goston burst into tears and pinged out of the room.

All the Heerajras chided the Younger, who exploded into a fit of laughter. The Elder sat back down.

"I do have a poem, Your Majesty," he quaked. "I-I can recite it to you, after the meal."

The Queen smiled, her eyes creasing. "I would love to hear your poem. I will need to find my daughter first. She moves as fast as lightning—"

Just as she moved her chair back an inch, Goston returned to the dining room, looking slightly flushed, and sat back on her chair, completely ignoring Polymir. Celd Dion, taking advantage of the opportunity, presented his black corn and bottle of oil to the Queen and the others. Iros gestured that the diminishing gold liquid she had brought was for the Queen also.

Celd Dion offered the food from his planet — which, to some of the Heerajras, was like eating a flavourless solid. The oil was thick and warm, completely foreign to the cooler liquids more familiar on the other planets. Heerajras fared better when eating their own food that they had materialised. Leifweiden smiled at Navas, who smiled back and playfully rolled her eyes.

"How is your art, Navas?" Leifweiden asked her.

She could feel the sketch rustle under her top.

"It's fine, thank you. Honestly, even a flower still has this beauty after all this time. There's always a way to capture its beauty."

"Maybe I can have a piece of artwork," said Leifweiden. "Maybe we all can?"

She nodded. "I'd love that. But I know Geadeous has her own artwork."

Geadeous had spent the entire dinner thus far glaring at the Queen. "Sweet Navas, you toil, and I materialise," she replied. "It's easier that way. I do like the easier life. Just to sit back and let others... fret. It seems fine."

The Queen narrowed her eyes.

Iros bit her lip and said, slightly slurred, "I can't have a painting. I have no room… or walls." She frowned, trying to remember her Kassel.

The Queen smiled politely and asked everyone how they were, whether they needed any more drinks. She particularly directed this question at Entanerus, who remained stock still. Navas wondered if Entanerus and the Queen could communicate without talking out loud. As the Queen directed a question to Celd Dion, Geadeous had to blurt out, "You've not asked me, Glaruntia. You have not asked *me* the trivial question of how I am."

"I am asking everyone, Geadeous. I am asking Celd Dion presently."

Celd Dion, finally addressed by the Queen, had nothing to say.

"You've not even looked at me all this time, at all," scoffed Geadeous.

"Stop this childishness, Geadeous." The Queen looked at Geadeous in anger.

Navas suddenly wondered if Geadeous would transform into a tyrant. She looked to Iros, who was now slumped in her chair. Princess Liras looked quietly annoyed.

"I am *not* one of your children," said Geadeous. Her voice was hard.

"Geadeous. I am being spoken to. I have not seen you in many years," Celd Dion said to her, and it threw her.

"Many years ago, we spoke on the bridge," recalled Geadeous. "We were much younger. Your plants were saplings. Many years have passed. Enough time to think. You have decided to speak to me over Glaruntia, Celd Dion. I'm impressed."

Celd Dion lit a cigarette. The smoke he breathed out gushed over the food. He sat back and smiled at Geadeous. Navas had never seen Celd Dion smile.

"You are so... *stormy,* Geadeous," he said sardonically. It was such a bad joke that Geadeous smirked back.

"My, my, Your Majesty…" breathed the Younger Polymir, who ate from the Elder's plate. The Queen didn't know whether to materialise another plate for them.

"I've not met Entanerus properly. Is he real?" Iros asked hazily.

Crooked Dancer was placing cutlery all around Entanerus, balancing everything carefully into little bridges. The Queen asked him politely not to do that and Geadeous shook her head, proving her point that Glaruntia was patronising.

It was Leifweiden's turn, and the Queen asked him about his studies.

"I have finished my observatory," he replied. "It's taken many years, but I can see so far out. It's beautiful, my Queen. Seeing out there, such colours and... the different planets are wonderful."

The Queen smiled. "What made you want to see further out?"

Leifweiden stopped smiling. "Years ago, I saw a red... smudge in our skies. It concerned me. But it went. I can only think it was an explosion. A star that had maybe lost its life."

The all-seeing Queen had seen it, too. But she had told no one.

"I'll protect you all, if there is a meteorite falling on us," Geadeous said proudly. "More than what a head can do… a face. A crown." Her voice became derisive. Princess Liras was about to speak, but the Queen simply raised her hand.

"Funny, my sleeves are going red. I can't seem to stop it," Leifweiden said absently. Everyone had heard him say this, but no one knew how to reply.

"It's gone now, then," continued the Queen. "You can watch our skies, Leifweiden, to help if there is any danger—" The Queen was interrupted by Geadeous, who said that she would do it better.

"Geadeous, it's not all about you," Leifweiden replied firmly.

Goston sat on her hands to stop them shaking.

"Ohhh, it's happening now…" Iros was almost falling off the chair, her words a long slur.

Younger Polymir laughed and Geadeous's skin flashed black. Navas couldn't stop her tiny little gasp.

"All of you are so in awe of this woman – but what has she done for us?" She slammed her fist on the table, the cutlery bouncing up into the air for a moment.

Leifweiden had to say to Geadeous that she should speak to the Queen directly. As he spoke, plasma burst so close to them that they could all hear it. The Queen realised her children would need to leave soon. She couldn't keep her energy *this* low for too much longer. Her mind wasn't calm.

"Geadeous," she said steadily. "You are powerful. But you cannot become a sun any more than I can become a planet. This gathering was a gift for me from our Princess. You are not happy with me, I understand. But I cannot make you shine as I do."

Geadeous's eyes became redder, and she bent a knife in her hand.

"Why not?" she replied. "You have so much energy to spare – this fire in the sky could lend some energy to me. You saw us all when we were born... surely, I was to be what you are?"

"I did not create me, did I?" The Queen was steel jawed now. "I cannot help you, no more than you can help who you are—"

"Stop speaking to me like I'm a child!"

"You are *acting* like one!"

A crash of plasma fell again, much closer this time. It sounded like the swell of a wave crashing. Leifweiden tugged at his scarf again.

Princess Liras was so angry at Geadeous. Navas observed her sister and was suddenly saddened.

"I'm leaving," said Geadeous. "This was a ridiculous visit. Your selfishness knows no bounds-"

She stood to leave, but Leifweiden held her orange wrist and said strongly, "*Stay*. Don't leave like this."

The Younger whistled. "This guy. He has no fear. Isn't that right, Elder?"

The Elder was entranced by what was going on. Navas was so proud of Leifweiden at that moment. She then looked at Princess Liras, who was upset as this should have been a happy occasion.

    Geadeous leant over to Leifweiden and whispered to him to never touch her again. Leifweiden released her wrist, but his eye contact never wavered.

Geadeous was so close to him, that Navas felt a little pang in her heart. Geadeous sat back down in her chair and folded her arms crossly. Both she and the Queen were taking deep breaths in order to calm down.

The Queen tried to be calm in most situations and hated that she had raised her voice to Geadeous. She had to set an example and was annoyed she was arguing over dinner, a party, and that Geadeous got a rise out of her. Glaruntia never forgot the first time she'd seen Geadeous. She wished she would act... more regal. Geadeous looked the part but could become incredibly bratty. Iros, on the other hand, loved seeing Geadeous angry.

Geadeous could cause some serious damage in her tyrant form.

Navas mouthed "thank you" to Leifweiden and he winked back at her. Crooked Dancer had now completed his little knife bridge creation on top of Entanerus. It had even survived Geadeous's outburst.

"I'm sorry I screamed at you, Polymir," Princess Liras said simply. "We are so apart. I'm lucky to be close to my sister. But you have made me realise that we need to be closer, so that we can help each other." She looked at Geadeous. "And we can talk, if needed. Instead of feeling alone."

Iros and Goston agreed, as did the Younger Polymir and Leifweiden.

Geadeous smiled at Princess Liras.

"Princess, I thank you." Geadeous glanced at the Queen, whose steely gaze didn't falter. "Perhaps there will be a day where there will be nothing more to say."

"A toast to the Queen," announced Celd Dion. He looked to Princess Liras, who held her glass high, and finished grandly, "And to our Princess." They all raised their glasses. As they did so, the sky became red.

The Red Light

The Heerajras all looked at Leifweiden who, in turn, looked at the Queen, who quickly looked out of the window.
Iros rushed over to the window itself. "I can hear something weird... like Heerajras?" She steadied herself by holding on to the windowsill. "What is it?" she asked the room.

Navas went to join Iros, as did the Queen and Goston, who was trembling more so than ever. She pinged to Princess Liras and sat in the Queen's vacated seat. Celd Dion had to do a double take at the sight of the little girl sitting on the giant head chair and thought it most improper.
However, they could all feel it.

The feeling of falling and one's stomach forming a knot. The pressure increased around them as well, and their hearing became muted, as if their ears needed popping.
The Queen listened and could hear mournful wails and screams, against a blasting noise like that of a blowtorch.

It became deafening, and any sound that The Sun was making was mixed with the ghoulish moans and cries. The Queen realised that the energy was only going to get hotter on The Sun, too.

The Queen took a breath. "Wait here. I'll see what it is…"

Geadeous stood and scraped her chair back. "I'll go. You are not our protector."

"We don't know what this is—" the Queen began.

Geadeous didn't falter and said forcibly, "*I'll* go."

Iros wanted to go with her but found herself edging closer to the Queen. Navas glanced over at Liras, who was trying her best not to look frightened.

I should get Liras somewhere safe, Navas thought quickly.

The Queen seemed to read her mind.

"We'll need to get to safety. Whatever it is, it's getting close."

Geadeous stepped out of the palace, out of the sky-high doors, and she saw a large, black semi-circle. She frowned. The wind and energy of the object blasted the air around her, and she transformed into her golden virago, her orange body encased in armour.

She couldn't understand what was in front of her. A black circle that blocked out the stars behind it and a red rainbow that had so much energy it was screaming and wailing. The rainbow was so large, that the red bands reached as far as Planet Entanerus. It looked like a fierce arc in the sky. The wind and energy from the black circle blew the hot air from The Sun and Geadeous narrowed her eyes more. She'd never felt this energy before. She tried to anchor herself on the ground, but she slipped due to the sheer weight of energy around her.

There was a long walk between the black circle and the palace doors, but she felt that at least there was some cover if needed behind the giant statues that lined the walkway.

Geadeous unsheathed her sword, and, from the centre of the black circle, there appeared glass red steps. They were produced quickly but were not close enough for Geadeous to step on them. The noise of the gale was becoming deafening. Geadeous gripped her sword tightly and watched the red rainbow, flashing with chasing light, particles and screaming comets. *What is this energy?* she wondered.

The others came out of the palace, but hung in the doorway and Geadeous yelled at them to get back in. The Queen's mind was in two – to determine if the red arch was a threat, or to hide her children away. She wanted Geadeous to get back to safety, too.
The younger Heerajras stood with Leifweiden and Navas and they gasped at the red, fizzing sight in front of them.
"What is that?" Iros yelled back to Geadeous. It was strange to see the sky blacked out.
"Get back, Iros!" Geadeous shouted over the noise.
Younger Polymir shouted back at her.
"There's someone there!"
Geadeous spun around.
At the top of the stairs stood a man in a red jodhpuri suit, tailored for a tight fit. He had long, black hair that flicked down to his cheekbones. He was a gorgeous man, similar in age and appearance as Leifweiden. Navas reached out to Princess Liras. She could see, despite the rushing of energy, that the man was gazing at Princess

Liras lovingly. His eyes were fixed on her sister. It unnerved her.

The Queen stepped behind Entanerus and placed her hands on his shoulders. She wanted everyone back inside.

"Oh, my beautiful." Despite the noise and distance, everyone could hear the man on the stairs as clear as a bell.

"Who are you?" Geadeous barked at him. She wanted to grow to the size of her planet, but whatever energy this man had, it seemed to quell her ability to do so.

"I am The Quasarjra," spoke the man. "This is my home, my palace, my chariot. I'm here for my bride. Not your old hand. You can put that blade down."

Navas didn't realise she could hold her sister as tight as she did. Leifweiden stood in front of the pair of them.

Celd Dion said to the Queen, "We should take the Princess back inside—"

The Queen, however, couldn't take her eyes off the man in red.

"I've been looking for you for so long," he said tenderly. "And then, in the blackness of space, I saw your light. It wasn't bold, but a sheen, the sheen of pearl." The Quasarjra's voice was as soft as velvet.

Princess Liras was speechless and the dread Navas felt became as painful as a punch to her gut. The Quasarjra looked so besotted, so transfixed by Princess Liras, as if she was indeed a true love of his.
As Navas held her sister, each jewel and diamond cut into her arms, but she wouldn't dare release her grip.
"Leave here, Quasar!" ordered the Queen. She stepped in front of everyone but Geadeous. "You are too strong for this world! You cannot talk to her. She isn't going anywhere!"
"I am *so* strong. I can eat you all in a second. I can destroy your little solar system." The Quasarjra waved his hand dismissively. "See, my rings are encasing you all." He didn't sound threatening, just irritated that he wasn't getting his own way.
Two blades appeared from his hands. They were the colour of vermillion orange, and fizzing hot energy blasted from the golden hilts.
Geadeous watched as The Quasarjra held the blades on either side of his body. The energy went on for miles, so

much so that Geadeous couldn't see where the blade tips ended.

The Heerajras were too close to appreciate how large The Quasar's body was. Its accretion disc went beyond Planet Entanerus and The Sun, and the entire solar system and beyond could fit comfortably within the disc. Sometimes, The Quasar resembled a red-winged bird as it travelled through space. Other times, it shrank the eye of its disc so that the red energy was all anyone could see, a furious red mouth with its two blades bursting out, a scythed chariot wheel boundless in the cosmos.

"Don't upset me, star," he said. "I am not here to fight, or yell. I am not leaving until I have the Princess. Don't make this harder. I have reined in my energy, you *know* this. Just as you do for your Heerajras. If I unleash my energy, you will *all* be sorry."

The Queen pulled a searing gold whip from under her robes. "You're not taking her."

The Quasarjra smiled as he looked down at the Queen. The younger Heerajras were indoors, peering from the doorway. The heat and sounds were getting louder to

Navas. They had already been on The Sun for too long and she felt her skin prickle with the heat. This man needed to leave them, and now.

She quickly looked down at Princess Liras, who was staring helplessly back at the Queen. "Liras let's get to a safe place. We have to take you and the—"

"I'm not leaving, star," said The Quasarjra curtly. "Let her go, and I won't fight you."

The Quasarjra shrank his blades so that they were more manageable to wield but were still as long as his legs.

He continued to direct the blades on either side of him, so that his hips looked horned. The Heerajras, heating up now, saw in a split second how the Queen waited for The Quasarjra to react. Her thumb pressed on the grip, and she launched the whip at him, the large, golden tail as fiery and bright as a solar flare. She managed to miss all the Heerajras, who were still standing by the palace entrance doors, and Geadeous, who still had her sword out, took a few paces closer to the stairs.

The Quasarjra reacted faster, however. He caught the whip in his hand and released it just as quickly, so that it snapped back to the Queen. She dodged the flare as it headed back to her. She was about to try and attack again, but The Quasarjra's left sword was now increasing in size and he was ready to attack the Queen. Before anyone could react, the large red effervescing sword was on its way to greet the Queen.

The Queen was pushed to the floor, and it took her a second to realise what had happened. Geadeous was in front of her and had shielded her from the sword.

"*Geadeous!*"

"I said – nothing will come to harm—" Geadeous tried to get up from her kneeling position, her left flank bleeding heavily.

Iros couldn't see what had happened, as Polymir was covering her, doing his best to not let the younger Heerajras see what was going on.

Leifweiden backed off towards Navas. Celd Dion stood by the large doorway, too. The Queen…

"What happened?" Goston blurted out, shaking into Iros. Goston wanted nothing more than to run away. Iros wanted to go see what was happening but heard a scrape of the sword.

Geadeous picked up her metal sword and held her left side. Her own body was fizzing and sparking red. Even where the sword had hit the floor of the palace, it seemed like the tiles were burning away. Her skin flashed from orange to black, as her tyrant form attempted to assist. Geadeous strived to stand but fell on her knees and the Queen rushed over to her.

"*Faster*, I need to get stronger!" Geadeous pleaded to her tyrant form.

Kneeling in front of her, the Queen examined the wound and, even in the red and yellow glow of The Sun and The Quasar, Geadeous looked a pale orange.

Geadeous swore under her breath. "I can't fall yet!" she despaired. This wasn't normal energy, like fire or metal or electricity. It was acidic gas, tightly knit into weapons.

The heat was increasing, causing the Queen to lose focus in her attempt to calm her energy.

"He's stopping us… from getting bigger or stronger…" spoke Geadeous. "My tyrant form—"

The Queen nodded in understanding. "He's been watching us. I don't have time to grow here, either. Save your energy, Geadeous. We must get to safety."
Leifweiden, seeing that this wasn't over, rushed past Geadeous and the Queen and ran towards The Quasar. "Leave, now! We're not here to fight!" he yelled at the untroubled Quasarjra.
"Leifweiden!" Geadeous called to him. "Don't engage with him."

They all watched as the accretion disc began to turn clockwise, accompanied by a ticking noise with each movement, as if The Quasar was revving up to a certain speed. Goston felt ready to faint and Iros, who wasn't exactly sober, tried her best to shield Goston's eyes while trying, at the same time, to see for herself what was happening. As Iros did so, she felt Goston slip from under her arm... They were all so enraptured by the red disc, that no one else noticed the missing girl.
Crooked Dancer, during all of this, was transfixed by the red clock face that the accretion disc had become.
". yhport a eb ot tnaw t'nod I" he said detachedly.

Entanerus looked to be glowing as he was so hot, his senses overloaded with what was happening around him. Having Navas visit him on his planet was enough excitement to last a lifetime.

Polymir the Younger turned to the Elder. "We need to get out of here!"

"Listen to your virago." The Quasarjra took a step down, his eyes boring into Leifweiden's.

Navas gripped onto Princess Liras from behind now. "Navas… what can we do?" asked Liras tensely. "I can go if it helps…"

"*No*, sister!" baulked Navas. "We'll get out of here soon. We'll find somewhere he can't find us!" She turned, looking for somewhere they could hide, but was terrified that The Quasarjra would attack the others. She looked back into the palace, its gold interior shining throughout. As she took a breath to run back inside, she turned once more to look at Leifweiden.

Navas watched Leifweiden take a step back, then lean in to get a closer look at the disc. Trembling, and phasing in and out of being, was Goston, who was on the first glass step of the portal. She was so scared, yet she had ended up in the last place she wanted to be.

"Goston? Get down from there!" Leifweiden yelled at her, perplexed as to how or why she had placed herself in danger. Goston could move incredibly fast, to the point of teleporting, but she was so scared that she was glitching in one spot. The Quasarjra smiled in bemusement as Goston was running away and frozen at the same time. Leifweiden rushed up to grab Goston off the stairs.

Celd Dion and Geadeous called Leifweiden back. However, as Goston was phasing, he couldn't lift her easily and so wrapped his arms around her from behind. "Goston, our droplet, we have to move!" he urged in her ear.

She was hyperventilating. "I… can't… move!"

The Quasarjra took one more step down and the accretion disc began to spin faster and faster, so that the winds that gushed around the Heerajras almost blasted them off The Sun. The ticking was incessant now and the noise was becoming maddening for the Heerajras.

The accretion disc became an irradiated red and The Quasarjra, whose hair was now blowing wildly, grinned and said defiantly, "The Princess will leave with me. There is nowhere you can hide. I can tear this star into ruins with just a yell."

The deafening sounds were now shaking the world around them. The decibels were getting louder, as loud as a jet engine, and the air heavier.

"Ice planet. You saw me as I approached. You felt fear…" The Quasarjra's voice was now audible only to Leifweiden. "If only your eyes could see what I truly was. They are not useful to you."

Leifweiden's beautiful eyes widened.

"They are wasted on you," The Quasarjra continued. "I should remove them… could I deny a man his vision of his beloved?" He smiled very slowly, his voice full of playfulness and malice.

Leifweiden stood in front of the phasing Goston. His stance was strong, fists clenched. "You have to leave."

"Once I have gotten what I want. And what you deserve for challenging me."

Leifweiden's ice-blue irises flooded with a red cloud.

Battling against the wind, Navas saw The Quasarjra pick up his blades and, within a second, had struck something. Her hair flying in front of her face made it hard to see, but when she had vision, she could see Leifweiden on his knees, head bowed, and she screamed out to him. Celd Dion rushed over to him on the long path, fighting the wind and energy, and dragged Leifweiden back towards the doorway of the palace. "Get inside, Navas!" Polymir the Elder yelled at her. She nodded and, as she turned, she saw blood spilling from Leifweiden's face.

His entire face was red.

Celd Dion was holding onto him and Polymir tried to push Navas inside, but she was in shock. She needed to see if Leifweiden was ok. She felt as heavy as stone, wanting to make sure Leifweiden could at least see her. Her chest was as tight as a fist. Polymir dragged Navas and Princess Liras inside and, for a second, the deafening noise was drowned out slightly. Polymir managed to haul one door closed, using all his strength to do so.

As quickly as she had disappeared, Goston was back in Iros's arms, blood smattering her skirt. Iros felt her heart skip far too many beats. Goston was mentally gone. Her eyes were unfocused and her body heavy with limpness. Even her mouth had become slack.
"Goston? Are you ok? Is Geadeous ok?" Iros asked, knowing she wouldn't get a reply. She fought back tears. Iros felt the energy leave her, as if her blood pressure was dropping. "Is anyone ok?" she asked vaguely. She wanted to run away, and she could run faster than anyone here. She was more precise than Goston, but would running away make any difference? Could she leave the others?
Entanerus looked terrified. Iros released Goston for a second, but that was all it took for The Quasarjra to blast the doors of the palace open, breaking their hinges. The Heerajras were pushed to the floor.

The rumbling around them increased and all the Heerajras could feel a pull inside of them as they attempted to stand up. Navas, inside the palace, kissed Liras's forehead hard.

"What is happening, sister?" Princess Liras whispered fearfully, her eyes glassy from tears. "We can run, can't we? He can't destroy my Queen's home?"

Navas also wanted to know what was happening. With Liras in hand, she peered around the doorframe, and watched as The Quasar's accretion disc became a mouth, white lightning forming fanged teeth.

The Quasarjra himself had his mouth open, his arms outstretched, blades as long as the solar system floating either side of him. The ticking became so loud, that each tick and tock was deafening like the heaviest of thunder cracks.

Geadeous stood and pushed the Queen away from her. "Get back inside!" She used her sword as a cane. "I'm not leaving without you!"

Geadeous shook her head. Half her flank had been eaten away from the fizzing energy of the blade. She needed to become her tyrant form, but her mind and body were not connecting. Fleetingly, she wondered what this monster knew of her.

Meanwhile, Celd Dion had his hand on the back of Leifweiden. They didn't make it inside the palace. His eyes had been cut, his grey skin white under the blood. Celd Dion didn't have time to be startled.

"We need to run, Leifweiden," Celd Dion said softly in his ear.

Leifweiden nodded. "I don't know where Goston is. She was in my arms." His voice cracked with pain. Celd Dion closed his eyes in distress. He saw his black cornfields. Oh, to be there right now.

Leifweiden stood up uneasily as the black mouth opened wider and wider. Particles, light and heat began to zip past him. His own scarf slid off him and Celd Dion almost lost his footing. Both men had a nauseating feeling they had lost all their weight.

"We have to run!" Celd Dion snapped and began to run, using two arms to support Leifweiden. However, the pull from the portal sucked him and Leifweiden in. When it tried to take Geadeous, the Queen anchored herself by coiling her golden whip around a statue, a tenuous brace for Geadeous to hold on to.

But it was futile.

The pull of The Quasar had already blasted the palace doors clear off, the palace entrance an open theatre. The Heerajras were now exposed to the hot, electric air.

The Queen watched in horror as Geadeous was pulled into the mouth of the portal, the gold whip loosening like a ribbon.

The Queen tried to reach out to her, but the shock of the air pull took Geadeous away too quickly. The Queen so wanted to become sun size, but her other children would be lost in her flames. With nothing to anchor her, she swayed and was taken into the mouth also.

Entanerus was next. Navas couldn't let go of Princess Liras. The others were taken, one by one, from inside the palace, screaming until they met the darkness of The Quasar's mouth.

Princess Liras was screaming into Navas's chest, and Navas felt her feet rise.

Navas was dragged in, just after Goston, Iros and Polymir, the sisters' connection snapping against the pull.

As Navas was taken in, she screamed and reached out to Princess Liras, who was unmoved in the palace entrance.

It went black for Navas.

There was such a shock of silence, it felt painful to her ears. It was so dark, she wanted to call out, but she had to hold her breath.

Akin to being underwater, she couldn't breathe. There was grinding and the sound of rocks being broken down, almighty creaks and snaps of mountains.

She opened her eyes and saw all the planets being slowly broken up. They were in the same positions as if they were in space, and it was silent under this water world. The Sun was there. The planets were either tiny at this point, or Navas was massive, as she could see the entire solar system being torn apart, like a horrendous movie being played out in front of her.

She watched, confused, as the planets dissolved and then were reorganised back into their present form, slowly, as if they were being recreated, enrobed in fire. *Were they inside The Quasar?* she wondered.

After hearing a final tick-tock, everything went white. It was so white that, even if she closed her eyes, it was just as white and brilliant. Navas covered her eyes with her palms, then felt a sudden rush of air.

Navas suddenly found herself back out of The Quasar. She was now away from The Sun and close to Planet Leifweiden. She was floating high and far enough away to see the majority of the planets. Her head spun. Was this reality now?

The planets were red and sore, back in their present forms. Even the glass bridge had shattered. The planets had no atmospheres, no clouds – just hot, red, lava-coated spheres, taking in more and more matter around them.

She coughed up glittery plasma. She could see she was on a sparkling shoreline that reached past and beyond their solar system. Navas stood up. She was floating in this space, but, due to force exertion, she moved as though she was on solid ground. She saw to her left that Glaruntia was unconscious, with Princess Liras safely under her.

Princess Liras spluttered and screamed, "The man is still here!"

Navas, who was covered in the heavy glittery plasma, crawled to Liras. The Quasarjra had now moved his vehicle just above the Royals.

He was on the last step of his glass staircase and was bending over the Princess, hauling her up from under the Queen, who was slowly waking up. Liras herself was drenched, her dress weighing her down. Princess Liras screamed again. The Quasarjra pulled her close to him and kissed her hard on her mouth. "Oh, you taste like silk!"

Navas tried to grab his leg, but she was so slick and weak from being in the plasma waters, that he simply stepped back out of her grasp.

"Oh no, please don't take my sister! Take me instead. You can't do this!" she pleaded, then coughed up more glitter and plasma.

The Quasarjra gripped Princess Liras, who was struggling to get out of his clutches. As Liras was oily from the plasma, The Quasarjra tied a red energy band around her waist and then over her mouth.

The Quasarjra smiled. "It's not you I want," he said to Navas. "It's this wonderful bride of mine. Don't worry, I will take care of her."

Navas heard Princess Liras's muffled screams as The Quasarjra pulled her with him as he climbed calmly to the top of the stairs and back to the portal.

Navas tried desperately to climb the stairs after him, but each glassy red step vanished before her as it reached the portal.

"Liras!" Navas called out to her gagged and crying sister as she disappeared into the blackness.

She watched helplessly as The Quasar itself shimmered once, a ripple of particles and energy, and slowly moved away from the solar system. The screams and howls were carried away as The Quasar vanished and Navas was left with the quiet rumble from the planets being reformed.

Navas sat back and leant on her arms. *What had just happened?* she asked herself.

She coughed up the last of the plasma and the shoreline of the glittery plasma slowly faded away. Glaruntia looked at her, still in a daze.

"Navas... what happened?"

Navas shook her head, unable to speak.

Glaruntia looked around her at the planets spinning slowly, the heat and lava cooling on their surfaces. "They're being reborn? Remade? It looked like this when I was younger." She stood and looked down at Navas, who was still staring out. "Where is everyone?" The Queen flicked the plasma off her sleeves in disgust.

Navas shook her head and began to cry. "He took Princess Liras." Glaruntia knelt and placed a hand on her shoulder. Glaruntia closed her eyes tightly and hung her head.

"I... he was a quasar," she explained. "They feed on stars. The darkest energy colliding with one another... it creates monsters."

Monsters...

"No, they're ok. I can feel it," said Navas. She felt determined, yet her voice was hollow. She was still in shock as to what had happened, but she focused on the next step. To get her family back.

"I have to help them," she said softly.

Glaruntia shook her head. How did The Quasar release the planets but not the Heerajras? And what did he want with Princess Liras? She swallowed a lump in her throat.

"I'll go," Glaruntia replied. "I can travel faster and farther." She didn't know what she was saying.

The Heerajras and herself had never left the solar system. She didn't know how long she'd last while away from her star, either, such was their energies.

The Quasar was so large that it could travel far and swiftly. Were they gone? She couldn't feel their energy anymore on their planets.

Navas stood and nodded. "I must get my sister back. You can stay here in case they return." Navas suddenly realised she was telling the Queen what to do.

The Queen realised this too and had to smile. "To find him in this world won't be easy. And there is danger out there. Black holes, like The Quasar, are hidden. They will take anything they need to if they can. Heerajras and stars, they're unthinking. They're lost stars."

Navas looked around to observe the giant, aching, hot planets. The crumbled glass bridge was slowly spinning around the planets, and she frowned. Floating closer, she saw that The Moon was on fire as well. The pearl sphere itself was white in heat and its layers were being pulled away in the fire. Navas felt faint, a heavy laceration in her heart. The Moon was always the pearl... unblemished and perfect.

She had to get her sister back. As a result of the ejection of the planets, The Moon was now orbiting at a much further distance from her own planet. Navas looked down at her hand and saw that there was still a small imprint of Liras's bangle on the skin of her palm. She was joined by the Queen. "You weren't here," said the Queen. "There, when the planets were being born. It was scary, chaotic, but so beautiful. You could see the heat calming to reveal these orbs of colour and movement. The greens and blues... it was worth the wait to see what these worlds would look like once the fires had cooled."

Navas nodded, not quite caring.

"Please, let me go," she appealed. "I want them back. I don't know what I can do. Trick him, talk to him, bargain. But I need to try."

"I don't want to lose you too," said the Queen.

"You won't. I'll bring them back." Navas smiled against the fire and noise behind her. "I won't let you down. Besides, I can't go home. It's on fire!"

The Queen smiled sadly. She touched Navas's cheek. "I *can't* let you. It'd be your doom."

"I'm going anyway," said Navas defiantly. "You can either help me or I can go and die trying."

"Navastratun."

Navas held the Queen's hand. She hadn't heard her full name for so long. The pull was too strong.

"She's my sister and our Princess. Here, take this." Navas pulled out the survived sketch from her cleavage and handed it to the Queen.

The Queen looked at the family portrait and had to breathe in hard, so she didn't cry. It was wet from the plasma but was drying quickly. She turned her head and watched The Moon pearl lose its sheen completely. They wouldn't be able to tell the damage done for an age.

The Queen then took off an iron ring she was wearing and placed it on Navas's left ring finger. "This will protect you from a lot of the damage out there, like a ward."
She then picked a ruby from a different ring and said, "Eat this. This will keep you warm. These precious stones appeared like flowers in my palace. They're incredibly special and protective." Navas swallowed the gem and shuddered as she did so.
"Wow, it's like drinking tea!"
Glaruntia saw that Navas was wearing her usual low-cut green top and blue skirt, which hung low on her hips. Typically, she was barefoot. Glaruntia took a small cape off her shoulders and placed it around Navas's shoulders. It was larger than she thought, so it hung around Navas's breasts.
"It's something, at least. Just in case it's too cold?" said the Queen.

Navas smiled. "Thank you." She spluttered a little laugh at the absurdity of their situation. "I have no idea where to begin."

Glaruntia smiled slightly. She wanted her family back safely. There was a chance Navas could find The Quasarjra.

The Queen closed her eyes and, after a beat, said, "If you focus, he may have left some particles. Of red. It's hazy, but follow it. You must go now."

Navas nodded and shuddered. "I'm so scared."

Glaruntia nodded. "So am I."

Navas gazed out in the direction of where The Quasar went. "I'll need to catch up." She took a long, deep breath in. "How could I let her go?" Her bottom lip wobbled, and the Queen shook her head.

"It was so sudden," she replied. "None of us knew what was happening. Tell Geadeous – tell her 'thank you' when you see her." The whip on her side shone and Glaruntia presented it to Navas. The whip floated in front of her.

"Stand on the end," directed Glaruntia. "This should work. I can launch you. Remember, you will need to stop yourself. It will use a lot of energy. You have to work hard against the pressure around you."

Glaruntia held her whip at one end in front of Navas and she released it, so that it suspended in front of her, becoming as hard as diamond, sparkling with energy.

Both beings grew to the size of their homes, Navas the size of her planet and Glaruntia the size of her star. Navas herself was dwarfed by the giant Queen. The fabric of her cassock was suddenly so magnified, Navas could see every thread of the cloth.

Navas made her way to stand at the end of the fire-bright whip and felt odd. This was madness. She wanted to go as soon as possible to find her sister, as well as hug the Queen and cry in her arms.

"Are you ready?" Glaruntia's voice boomed.

Navas wanted to find Leifweiden. To tell him what she was about to do. His smile… "Yes, I'm ready." She yelled back.

On a turn, the Queen flicked the solar flare, which immediately reverted into its whip state and launched Navas into outer space.

Navas bulleted towards The Quasar, dodging anything that would impede her chase.

As Navas hurtled into nothingness, past the fiery planets, the stars became sharp bright lines and, before she knew it, she was far from home.
Beneath her, as she soared, she could see red particles as bright as stars that became thin red lines. She snapped herself back and stopped sailing through the sky, the world around her catching up to her in a dizzying whack. She panted and looked behind her. The energy alone that brought her to that point, winded her, her surroundings catching up with her in a heavy bearing.
She couldn't see her solar system anymore.

Glaruntia went back to her home palace and sat on the highest skyscraper.
Her robes flowed against the heat, and she closed her eyes, taking in the sounds of rumbling and destruction of her home. The planets were being recreated, yet her home was losing its hold. She opened her eyes and could feel tears running down her cheeks. As she looked down

at her robes, she only now noticed the blood of Geadeous. She heard rubble falling and glass shattering and could see her palace from the skyscraper. It was crumbling and falling into The Sun, a gold lake that was slowly absorbing her palace. She herself was undamaged and couldn't remember if The Quasar had taken The Sun in and spat it back out.

It happened so quickly, she realised, frowning. Why did she let Navas go? Why didn't she take her place? Glaruntia stared into space, unthinking, her mind trying to arrange what had happened. She tried to convince herself it had happened so quickly, too quickly, and that's how The Quasar had won.

She gripped onto Navas's sketch tightly, a raft in the rapids, just happy to have a physical reminder of family.

The Journey

Navas was now following the red particles at a more sedate pace. Moving through space was like moving through water. The Heerajras were always surrounded by energy and there was always an opposing force around them.

They could sit on the force, rest, walk and swim through it. For Navas, it was easier to move on her planet, to walk on the solid ground as opposed to floating, but walking around did still exert energy. Navas didn't swim through space as she would through water, but she had to propel herself through the apparent emptiness, kicking her legs gently.

    She stopped and rested for a moment. She had to be careful and not to overshoot finding The Quasar. Although space was massive, it moved so swiftly. She had never been this far out before, and it was so unfamiliar here. She had to take a moment to digest what she was experiencing. The sky from her world at night was as black as coal and the stars studded the emptiness. But, out here, The Void had barely any of its original colour. There were soft hues of pinks and greens and subtle blue clouds that broke up the blackness.

Navas was surprised to see so little black and so much colour. It was as if the coloured gases had torn through the blackness, roughly and unaided. Despite the seemingly feral light peering through the black, she was grateful for the colour around her.

    The stars shone brighter out here and were sharper somehow, shaped as wheel spokes and not dots of light. There were so many, she couldn't quite comprehend how the skies around her could fit any more stars in. To Navas, they would now become suns – or, at least, orbs of warmth and light.

In the air, she could hear muted bells, as if they were being rung underwater. It was beautiful to listen to. She closed her eyes and felt vulnerable and alone, yet completely in awe. If she listened carefully, she could hear very quiet wind chimes, twinkling. She could hear comets shooting around her, as well. Little chirrs and metal scraping behind the lighter sounds of bells.

There was excitement in her at seeing the world beyond her atmosphere.

She was terrified, as well, but the artist in her was absorbing everything around her. Red stars were now palm-sized in the distance, rather than drops in her night sky, and harder bodies like planets were visible, sailing past their suns. Galaxies hadn't come into focus just yet, but she wanted to think that the stars, with their soft, comforting glows, were homes to other Heerajras like herself. She hoped that, if she were ever to get lost, she could ask for aid.

Navas smiled in appreciation. The planets at home were beautiful, as was their night sky. Being out in this world was as though a veil had been lifted in front her. She had seen the arch of space from the bridge, but, from its vantage point, there wasn't anything close enough to bring into such clarity.

Navas travelled on. She had no idea when she would meet The Quasar out here. Fear and determination mixed equally in her. Navas didn't know what further out would look like; she'd only ever reached the outskirts and wasn't prepared to see such soft and gentle colours. Were she to observe this in her own night sky, she didn't think she'd ever stop painting.

Onwards she pressed.

After a time that Navas felt had passed, a soft fog of magenta and pink gases around her shifted her colour spectrum.

Only from this subtle colour change did Navas realise she was even travelling forwards. There was no wind for her to hear or feel. Nothing otherwise changed in her peripheral vision.

The foggy magenta gas felt damp and cool to her, a post-rain feeling on her cheeks.

The stars seemed to dim slightly, and in this fog, there was suspended red glitter. When Navas reached out to touch it, the glitter vanished. She floated for a moment, hanging in space. It was calming, and she looked in front of her for the red trail and could see it faintly, a sparkling beckoning to her family.

As she travelled on and followed the trail, the fog around her became thicker and damper, so that her hair blew up from the moisture and then stuck to her nape.

The fog created a tunnel, tall enough for her to stand in, but the walls of the fog became a pulsating tube the further she went in. She touched the sides of the tunnel. Navas felt her heart skip a beat. She turned back and saw that the exit was clear enough, a tunnel leading back out to the depth of space.

As she followed the red trail of light, she could hear a beat. It sounded like a heartbeat and the walls became pinker and transparent, like she was now crawling through a sunlit vein. Particles flew past her, and the air felt heavy, like soup, to the point she became drenched, but there was no liquid around her. Ahead of her, up through the vein, far enough for her to view it safely, was a tiny pinprick of light.

Curiosity made her follow this light, as it was so small. She hoped she could find out what was in this depth; it could be a clue to finding the red monster.

It was a longer walk than she realised, and it was getting hotter. Her clothes stuck to her limbs and her forehead was shiny. Her hair was unforgivable, such was the volume and coarseness. When she took a second to look back, the exit was gone.

She'd gone this far in... sweat was dripping into her eyes, yet she was too far in to turn back now.

On and on she went through the tube, her feet pushing into the unfamiliar fleshy sponge. The light seemed to increase in size, and she had a better view as to what it was.

Two light beams were spinning, one from each of its poles, like the lighthouse back on Planet Goston. Navas watched intently. It was beating like a heartbeat, as each turn of the light beam pulsed light through the foggy, illuminated veins. She hoped the beam of light wouldn't swoop over her.

Navas crawled closer and she watched the orb rotate.

It was tiny.

It was the same size as The Moon. Compared to The Quasar, it was so small, but the light was strong enough to shoot out of the fog. The clouds and fog around the small orb rippled and pulsed with the light so that the magenta fog looked beautiful to Navas. The light didn't escape the fog externally and she frowned. The light looked as heavy as metal.

She climbed closer and closer to the orb and then she felt the pull. The energy ripples were now physically felt, like gusts of winds passing her. The cape around her neck fluttered and was drawn towards the orb. She didn't notice as it stretched out slightly, becoming longer. She gasped. Was this a black hole? Navas touched her chest. She instantly remembered the smirk from The Quasarjra.

Another enemy? Stars themselves weren't safe here…

It was such a small light, but its energy reached out as far as it needed to. Navas wanted to leave, but the ripples of energy that surged through her body were strong, and the long, straight lights entranced her as they spun so passionately. Her hair, and even eyelashes, became longer as the energy of the pulsar star beckoned her to reach closer to its heart. Even her nails grew in length. Navas felt her skin pinch, and her lips become hot. Soon, her skin was feeling scratchy, as if sharp needles were being dragged over it. It felt dangerous being here, but she wanted to stare.

The beating rhythm was hypnotising.

She'd have to carry on for another length of time before she could touch it… as she stared, a drop of sweat darted from her forehead towards the pulsar. Navas had to leave.

She reluctantly backtracked and climbed all the long way out of the vein, the cold of space slapping her face hard. She breathed in deeply and turned around. The fog had captured her.

As she looked around, she realised the orb had vanished. It was as though the fog light had only revealed itself once she was in it.

Navas felt foolish, easily swayed. *I need to be careful*, she thought. She couldn't allow herself to be enamoured by a passionate light. She felt uneasy, as if the light was calling her to get closer. It seemed so devious to her.

She shook her head. The red trail led through the wavering-coloured fog. She'd have to go around it, as fast as she could. Navas didn't know if she should have stopped so soon or bolted further through space, but she wanted to see The Quasar before its driver saw her.

Navas swam on her journey. The red trail wasn't as strong now, as she had to take the longer way around. She wondered if The Quasarjra could simply ignore the dancing light. She wondered if they were of the same kin, luring innocents around them.

She floated past more nebulae in the cool space. They looked fragile, hanging in the sky like pinned, dead butterflies. She knew they were large, and she was far enough from them to observe them in their entirety. *Had my family seen this?* she wondered, as they passed here on the red chariot.

Did Leifweiden make a note to tell her, when they saw each other again? Was he wary of the black holes as well, like The Quasarjra's disc of energy? The man who saw her sister from such a distance.

Navas stopped and hung her head. Her stomach fluttered and she wanted nothing more than to hug her sister.

As she passed peculiarly coloured planets, giant swollen stars and sparkling comets, she remembered Geadeous. Although she was wounded, she could still become a tyrant. Navas felt slightly more reassured. Her family had a defence, wherever they were. She didn't know if the monster, the red bird in the sky, held her family in its mouth, along with Liras. They had Geadeous for protection, for now. Geadeous would find a way to break the chains and help them until Navas got there. *I'm on my way*, she thought determinedly.

Glaruntia had salvaged some items from the party. Her palace seemed to be resisting the burning of its erosion. She had an ear of corn from Planet Celd Dion and the sketch from Navas. She didn't even want to look at it, so she placed it under her chasuble, secured under her collar.

She wondered if she should visit the planets, but she decided to let them be born anew. Glaruntia closed her eyes tightly. Why didn't she fight harder? What did the red beast want with Princess Liras? Her Sun ached and hissed under its deconstruction.

    She floated from it and sat on a little rock, watching as the planets were remade. She wondered if this was the first time The Quasarjra had taken life like this, or was he mad from his creation? He seemed to know what he was doing.

Glaruntia watched her cape flow just beyond the edge of the solar system, no longer shortened for practicality, and listened to the creaking, storminess of their home. It was such a contrast from the peaceful stillness that existed before the red giant's visit.

The planets didn't seem to be vulnerable while they were being built. If anything, they seemed to be determined, eager to be completed, shrugging off energies and matter like excess garments. Glaruntia saw this and looked out, hoping to see Navas come back soon. She doubted if she could ever forgive herself if Navas didn't return with, or without, the others.

Navas continued to follow the red dust, and it glittered slightly dimly now. The Quasar travelled so fast, and in this space, she pondered the owner setting up home on another planet.

He'd seen her sister from so far away, and she wondered how he was capable of hiding. Perhaps he would turn off his energy, just as the stormy clouds could hide The Sun in her sky. Going from red to black to hide from stars and telescopes.

Navas shuddered.

The Quasar hadn't even shown his true power, and she winced at his bitter kindness to dim himself, just so he could take her sister from their Queen.

Navas gazed at the stark bright stars and wondered if they themselves were kings or queens. She wondered if the stars were alone or if they had families, too. She wondered if the other moons were at risk from The Quasarjra, and if he had moved through space trying to pinpoint the one he wanted.

No, Navas had to admit to herself. She stopped where she was floating. The Quasarjra was completely enamoured with her sister.

She stretched out and, just as she was about to move on, she heard a baby cry.

She looked around but could see nothing that might have made that noise. She didn't want to get distracted, as she was on the red path, left by The Quasar, her only road to her family. Again, she heard the same cry, which was met with another.

She couldn't have imagined it. There wasn't a planet near enough for a Heerajra to have made that noise, let alone that loud. Navas closed her eyes to try and focus on the source of the crying.

The only place the sound could have come from was the soft, green fog away from the red path, far into the distance, a little plumage of clouds. She couldn't let babies be alone out here…

The fog was further than she thought, but Navas figured she could go backwards to rejoin the path again. The red path was her course, she decided, and she would use it to judge her surroundings. She wasn't quite used to the distances out here, but as long as she had the red glitter *behind* her, she knew where she was – although, she wasn't entirely certain.

Navas floated towards the crying – and hoped it wasn't a baby – Heerajra. How in the world could it have ended up out here? She imagined a little baby all alone… she had to help it.

As Navas neared the green fog, it became denser and pricks of light became bright, sharp and piercing, their glare becoming long, thin spikes. The fog soon became thick mounds, but ever sparkling, like the waters back home. If The Sun hit her ocean's water just right, the dancing sparkles could be blinding. Over a large mound of almost solid fog and cloud, Navas saw a large bright orb, with a faint disc of particles and light set amongst it.

It was a baby star, she realised happily. Relief swept over her.

The orb gurgled and cooed, and she saw five others, all laid out in cribs, as if they were in a nursery. The babies were crying and rolling slightly in their beds.

"You're all so cute!" Navas looked down into their deep cribs from over the high walls. The orbs were small enough for her to hold in her arms. However, she didn't want to pick one up, just in case she dropped it.

As she peered over each crib wall, a sparkling green tendril of fog left the ceiling and rocked the cribs.

"Oh, these babies are so cute!" Navas said happily. "I thought it was one of us!"

The babies cried harder.

"Speak softly," the foggy tendril said in an authoritative voice. As the tendril spoke, the sparkles in the fog dimmed and brightened. "They need sleep and food, constantly. It's all they do. Sleep and eat. I speak as the Matron."

Navas couldn't believe these small spheres would become giant stars, large enough to own an entire solar system. At some point, her Queen had been this small, and maybe she had been looked after by the same Matron?

"They are lovely," Navas whispered. The tendril split and soon all six babies were being rocked at the same time.

"What are you doing here, Heerajra?" asked the Matron. "This is far for a planet owner to be."

Navas nodded, unsmiling. "A... Quasar. It visited our solar system and took my friends and family. My sister... I'm on a path to follow it."

"I didn't think those red beasts were that smart," the tendril replied loftily.

A red beast. It fit his profile perfectly. The black holes stole light from around them, Navas contemplated. The Matron, she speculated, raised stars only for them to be taken by, or become, black holes. The Queen had spoken to Princess Liras about life cycles, but it was a long time ago.

She had heard that black holes were bad, lifeless destroyers. Navas was glad that the Queen would teach Liras what she knew, so that Navas had an idea of what was around her. She wondered if Entanerus had ever known there were other planets surrounding him, let alone what dangers were outside his home.

The Queen herself must have seen the star patterns change over time, births of stars and the deaths as well. "You should be careful, Heerajra," said the Matron. "Stars are all-seeing. They can aid or maim. I didn't see a quasar pass here."

Navas nodded. She almost fell into a crib while stroking one of the babies, its light wonderfully warm and comforting. The baby happily threw up plasma and particles on her hand. Navas suddenly realised that her fingernails had grown longer. She frowned, wiped her plasma-soaked hand on her skirt and smiled at the baby, as it babbled away.

"Are any planets born this way?" Navas asked.

"Planets are born from the stars," explained the Matron. "Their stars may have planets, they may have many children, or just a few. Heerajras like yourself are then born from the planets. Stars, in turn, need to look after you, for as long as they can, just as I look after these stars."

Navas smiled softly.

"My precious stars," continued the Matron. "I'll look after you. No one shall eat you whilst I'm here."

As Navas lowered her hand towards a baby star, it shone brighter and both beings felt each other's warmth. The light from the baby star lit up Navas's face, so that her yellow eyes were illuminated. "You're so beautiful," she cooed. "Please grow to be goodhearted and strong." She spoke so softly; the Matron was touched.

The baby star fell asleep, along with the succouring light, and Navas's face was dimmed.

She felt honoured that her Queen was so kind and caring. Liras must have known this, too. "I should keep looking. Thank you."

The tendril clinked on the bright lights and played a little lullaby for the babies, who all fell asleep.

Navas could have stayed here longer. She wanted to stay with the babies and find out more about her world, but feared she'd never leave. The lullaby was so soothing, she wanted to curl up amongst the clouds and fall asleep as well. She hadn't known that the nursery was so close, and she decided she would show Princess Liras when she returned home.

"Take care, Heerajra," warned the Matron. "Some lights can harm. Remember that."

Navas nodded. She wanted to ask if these stars would become monsters. But then, how was the Matron to know?

"I understand…" said Navas. "I'll be back to see the babies." The green fog lifted a few shades brighter.

"We'll be here," replied the Matron.

Filled with content from the calming green of the nursery, Navas set out to find a star to help her. Perhaps they would harm her…or join forces with her. She had found the red trail and felt confident she was getting used to her surroundings.

She frowned, however. After some time, the red sparkling trail became fainter. She narrowed her eyes. "Oh no…" She spun around, looked up and down for the trail, but there was nothing. "Oh no," she said in despair. "No no no. I need this."

Her heart suddenly skipped a beat, and she began to panic. There was nothing near her to help her on her journey. She breathed in deeply and tried to calm herself down. Without the trail, she was lost. There wasn't a planet or star near her to even help her. Even the nursery was out of sight. She had spun around enough to confuse herself even more now.

How could she be this stupid? She hoped she'd simply taken a wrong turn.

She was alone in this space, her guide completely vanished.

There wasn't time for this. Navas reached her arms out slightly, as if to steady herself and soothe her racing heart in her dreadful situation. She didn't remember even moving *forwards* for the red light to go.

After looking in all directions, she closed her eyes and tried to feel her family's energy. It was all she could do.

She had to picture them, one by one, at the dinner, a place where they were all last together. There, deep in her heart, Navas felt the pull of another Heerajra's energy. It felt like a blurring vibe, a tenuous spider's web in her being. She sighed with relief. It worked!

As she moved forward to follow the very slight pull of her family, she suddenly heard a rumble in the distance, a hum of energy getting louder and closer to her. She could also see a glint of light in the distance ahead of her.

The hum was getting louder and louder, and she had a horrible feeling it was The Quasar. Or perhaps it was just the energy of the world around her... She clasped her hands over her chest and looked about her frantically. Navas had to hold on to the feeling of her family, in case she lost it. Without that and the trail, she'd be completely lost.

The rumble was getting louder, and the light appeared brighter, too, but Navas still couldn't see a source for this energy. She guessed it was a stronger star in the distance, which she assumed was causing the light effects around her.

Navas drew her hands tighter into her chest and dropped her chin. Eyes tight, she kept thinking of her family, over and over again, desperate to hold the energy sensation she'd felt. She lifted her knees to her chest and refused to let anything distract her.

A hiss was closing in on her. It was no louder than the sound of a geyser back home. It was getting closer to her, but not louder.

Navas closed herself into a ball.

With her back to the energy source, she wouldn't have seen it wasn't The Quasar.

On a lost orbit, a large blue star was hurtling towards her at a great speed. The blue star was so large, it was on the same level as her own planet compared to the Sun, yet her Sun was the Planet Navas in this scenario. Only when the hiss and the pull of its gravity reach affected her did she turn around.

Navas almost fainted. The light was blinding. She froze, in space, watching this mountain of a star hurtle towards her.

The blue star moved so rapidly, and it was so large, she couldn't move out of its way fast enough. The gravity pull hit her from such a distance that the star's heat didn't even reach her until it was much closer to her. Navas tried to move, swim, run, but the gravity pulled her in harshly, her voice lost as her lungs winded her. Desperately, she tried to escape the pull of the energy, but it was useless. She felt a great rush of heat, and, after a slap of pain, it all went white for her.
Navas felt like she was on fire, and her clothes were singed.
She found herself in a completely white room, lying on a soft floor that felt like a melting sponge. She became hot rapidly and any contact her skin had with the white surface burnt her immediately. She tried to float but couldn't pull away from the floor.
"Help me!" she screamed. She quick-footed up, but the heat was too much. She fell to the ground, burning her sleeve and skin. Navas's eyes began to water. *It can't end here*, she told herself. She knew that the star must be moving her further away from the trail.

Her breath was shortening, and her skin was becoming tender and sore from the heat around her. It was so white she had to close her eyes tightly to bear it. Even still, she saw red behind her eyelids. The atmosphere felt light, and a crackle and pop was heard as though a speaker was being turned on.

Above her, a large human eye appeared. It had a blue iris and took up the entire ceiling. Navas screamed when she saw the one giant eye.

"A Heerajra!" a female voice exclaimed and, instantly, the temperature dropped. The voice echoed throughout the room and bounced back to Navas from the corner less walls. It sounded like the voice was speaking through an old microphone, and Navas was listening through a fuzzy speaker. It was still hot.

The heat was permeating her insides, but she could at least tolerate the contact she had on the surface. Navas lay on her back, gathering her breath. Her palms and soles were burnt, and her clothes were charred. At least the heat was quieter.

"What is this? Where am I?" she said out loud. Bearing in mind how fast the star was moving, Navas wondered if she was now just too far from The Quasar.

As she looked up, she felt nauseous, and her head began to throb. She hauled herself up to stand upright and she clutched her head. "Can you help…" Phases of blackness filled her eyes and she retracted into a foetal position, her cheek on the ground. "Any… one…" As Navas closed her eyes, she felt a comforting warmth and felt like she could sleep forever. It felt unusual for her, as if she'd fallen asleep on a tabletop rather than her bed. She wanted to sleep, but she wasn't in the right place. As she had her eyes shut, she could sense the light had changed.

"Who are you?" she asked groggily.

"Such a small planet." The female voice spoke in a simple childish way, despite the voice sounding like it belong to an adult.

Navas took a deep breath. "You're too strong for me. Let me go…" Then she thought to herself that it might be ok to sleep here… She was so tired. The blue eye stared down.

"I am large. I am dying."

"Why are you dying?" Navas spoke breathlessly, her energy draining quickly. Now she felt like she was in her oceans, warmed by the lava. It felt safe to sleep, and she wouldn't drown. *This is much better*, she thought dreamily.

"I am so large, I'm on fire," began the eye. "It hurts, like a gnawing ache all over me. This pain is tearing me up inside."

Navas struggled to even answer the eye. "You're a star... a white or blue star?"

The blue eye narrowed and blinked, the lid glaringly white. "I used to be a sun, now I am a star. I grew too big for my solar system. I had twenty children and... I... became too angry. There was an accident. I circle the world, waiting for my energy to run out."

"Can you let me sleep?" asked Navas. "I feel like you're draining me."

"You can sleep, but you will get lost in my white," said the eye aphetically. "You will dissolve into me, and I'll take you where I took my children."

Navas had a recollection of Liras sitting against a tree trunk, dappled by sunlight, in the woods back home. "No!" She propped herself up on her arm. "I need to find the red Quasar! He has taken my friends!"

The eye's pupil dilated, and it said innocently, "Are you sure you want to sleep? You can stay with me as I fall apart. We are so far from anything like a Quasar. I can send you backwards, but you will need to find your way. What a villain, getting so close to your home! Quasars, our houses, which have fallen into disrepair."

Navas stood, but screamed out as her feet were burning, so she fell back to her knees. She had no idea what the sun or star was referring to, but it seemed to be speaking simply, not at all adult like the Queen. "Hurry, please, I *need* to get out of here!" pleaded Navas.

"Your home is very unusual," said the eye. "One star, one moon. You hold the iron from your little star. You hope your star won't become an animal. The Quasar is as large as all of you combined, with many children and mothers and fathers and homes. He can see across our starry plain. Fear not, planet, you will get your friends back."

Navas looked around her and sat, clutching her knees, her skin being burnt by the acidic heat of the star. She resisted sobbing. She could only assume it was the little iron ring that was protecting her. This sun must have lost all control in its solar system. Perhaps its heat wasn't in control, either?

The star asked Navas to step through her eye.

Navas closed her eyes. It was so white and calming. So calming that she felt sleepy. She hoped she could muster the energy to escape this place.

She clenched her burnt hand into a fist. Stop getting drawn in, she scolded herself.

Navas raised her hand to reach up towards the brilliant blue eye. Her burnt soles ached, and her skirt was burnt to knee length now. Even her hair had been burnt away. "Think of your family. I will think of mine, I always do. All my children," the star said happily. However, the radio voice grew slower, until the blue star sounded like a deep-voiced monster, the speakers crackling and the eye dilated. The pupil began to expand over the entire iris.

Navas felt a wave of fear looking up at this black abyss. As Navas held her shaking hand up, she heard a latch break. She spun around to see that the bottom of the star had given way to a deep abyssal blue. One plank at a time was being dropped into the blue, reaching steadily towards her.

"Hurry, please." said the eye in its polite monster voice. "The floor is giving way!"

The eye's voice was so slow that it became a deep resonance. Above the deep voice, Navas could hear urgent whispers and suddenly felt her heart cave in. The temperature increased. Drenched in sweat, her clothes catching alight from the fierce heat, along with her hair, Navas screamed to the star. "Help me, please!"

The whispers of "help" surrounded her, like dancing fragments of wind, but she covered her ears. "Oh, poor little planet. Join my lost little children…"

The eye's voice was completely void of emotion and was as deep as the bellows of the volcanoes back home. "Let me mourn you, as I did a very long time ago…"

The deep voice began to sob, each release of sound mixed with other Heerajra's shuddering for air.
Before the last plank could be dropped, a giant drop of purple plasma fell from the eye and landed on Navas.

The impact was so strong, it was like a boulder hitting her body. The force of the plasma ejected her from the star, propelling her into space. Navas surely hit asteroids and was close to hitting planets, but she was as fast as a bullet and shot through the debris, each knock and bump a painful collision for her. Fortunately, she didn't smack into any planets, but the asteroids and rocks all took their toll on her.

She had to stop.

The asteroids were beginning to slow her down and it took all her energy, willpower and might to stop herself from flying through space, and she felt the entire space behind her catch up with her, with a rush of wind as she stopped. If the Heerajras had no internal energy, it would be impossible for them to stop their momentum.

As Navas's surroundings caught up with her, her entire stomach knotted and almost came up out of her mouth.

She caught her breath. She was winded and confused and had no idea where she was. Her entire body ached, and she was left with bruises and cuts from her ejection. At least the coolness of space was easing her pain from her burns. She shook from the aftermath of her expulsion.

Navas looked back at the star and was astonished to see how large it was. It must have been moving at great speed to explain the surprise of it appearing on the horizon. She hoped the Queen never left their home, a running beast without its family. *Would our Queen even hurt us?* she wondered. *Hope your star won't become an animal...* Navas felt a throb in her heart. Her Queen wouldn't hurt them. The blue star had children, too...

Navas didn't want to think about it. She just wanted to escape to her studio and paint, to remain ignorant of this torment beyond her home.

Navas could see that her feet, clothes and hair had been charred. She remembered the small rock she kept in her cleavage and tried to materialise more clothing. It didn't work. She stared hard at the little rock and realised the energy of her home was different since The Quasar... her eyes became glassy.

She felt bare and was thankful for the cape her Queen had given her. She pulled it tighter around herself. How was it possible that the star did not vaporise her?

The iron ring... she looked down at it on her finger. Navas shuddered at the thought of being without its protection. Her skin felt so raw and sore. She relaxed in the coolness of space, if only for a moment, and her eyes closed. She stretched out her fingertips and toes, her neck craning up. It felt good to stretch, but how everything hurt.

She opened her eyes slowly.

Keep going.

Navas could no longer see the red trail, but she had to carry on with her journey regardless, moving in the opposite direction to the blue star.

She tried to feel her sister's presence, but there was nothing.

She followed her gut instinct as the world around her became slightly darker, and the sharp bright gems of stars seemed dimmer somehow. As Navas floated on to get her bearings, she frowned.

She could see stars, but they were far away and faint, like how she saw them from home. The skies were darker, and the coloured fog and gases were all but gone. She had gotten used to the coloured ink splashes in the black skies.

She couldn't hear the bells, either. It felt colder in the air. Navas realised there was no sound at all. She frowned. Everything felt dimensionless to her, as if she was in a painting. On her planet it made sense. She could feel the grass (on the ground), see the mountains in the distance. She could see sky (above her) and she knew, if she went deeper into the waters, it would grow darker. Being out in space was odd to her. The stars looked flat, there was nothing in front of her, and above was the same as in front... behind was the same, but it wasn't and there was no floor. There wasn't a sparkle of red light, either.

Navas touched the Queen's cape. She was beginning to get confused. At home, it was straightforward, and everything was in its place. But here... she was chasing a chariot that knew this otherworld. She suddenly felt frustrated and very much alone.

She drew her knees up to her chest and buried her face in them.

"Dear sister…" It became colder as Navas floated on.

How long had she been gone? How long had her sister been out here in this empty chasm? There was no night and day to anchor time anymore.

Her fingertips began to feel hot and then freeze over, her toes becoming numb. She hugged her knees harder. Her eyelashes became white as they froze. Navas closed her eyes and tried to imagine a warm evening on her planet. Princess Liras and herself in the ocean, splashing each other, the water sparkling with white glitter under The Sun.

Navas opened her eyes. It was almost black. She felt the coldness over her eyes and a very blurry image of her sister appeared before her. If she focused, she could see Princess Liras again on Planet Navas, watching the tulips sway in the wind, completely unaffected and safe.

Snap out of this, Navas, she thought desperately. *Your sister…*

Navas was cold, and it was so silent she could hear her own heartbeat. As the ice over her eyes became thicker, her sight dimmed to a point where everything was closing in on her, with just the faint shape of her blurry knees visible. Yet, she could feel her eyes were still open.

Why can't I feel anything? she wondered.

Very faintly, she could hear a bell or two and a chime in the far-off distance. The blue star tried to help, she reasoned. Navas's head felt heavy, and she couldn't move anymore.

"Oh, sister," she sobbed internally. And it went completely black for her.

As much as she couldn't see anything, Navas could still hear. She felt a deep warmth in herself, despite being frozen on the outside. In her mind's eye, she felt comforted to see Princess Liras back at home and, one by one, the rest of her family joining her on the grassy plains, smiling and waving to her. She tried to join them, but her vision was too blurry. She felt herself fall onto the grass but couldn't get back up. Her family didn't rush over to help. She could see a fan of blurry, green grass in front of her eyes that slowly darkened.

Navas, in reality, frowned slightly. She had to remember where she was. She wasn't at home and her family were not on her planet. They never had been... Her lips were stone cold and her toes purple, as hard as rocks. She could feel the burning of the ice forming over her. It was too cold even for the ruby to fight back the frigid temperature.

As she floated alone in space, amongst the distant sparkling stars, she felt someone hug her from behind her, their cold and hard arms embracing her over her shoulders. The arms she felt were colder than ice.
I can feel this?
Her heart beat so hard in her panic that her eardrums throbbed.
Someone was out here with her. Navas suddenly felt a rush of water that immediately melted the ice around her. She spluttered, only to find she couldn't breathe. The waters around her were murky, filled with debris and

particles, like rainwater washing over mud. She turned around in the dirty waters to face a skeletal Heerajra, still embracing her. Navas tried to scream, but she couldn't. All Heerajras could breathe in space and water, but this chemical liquid she was in was taking all her breathing capability. The Heerajra scraped and bit at her, causing her neck to become bloodied, her blood clouding the waters.

Navas tried to look for an exit but, in the distance beneath her, all she could see were dying or dead planets. Even dead stars were deep beneath her, white and black dwarfs being dragged through the chemical waters like conkers on strings.

Navas was running out of air. Around her, many skeletal Heerajras grabbed her and reached out to her, their voices deep, sorrowful wails. Their fingers still had fragments of skin that floated and broke off into the waters. Navas tried to fight them off, as her own skin and clothes were being torn apart. She couldn't move easily, no matter how hard she tried – the water was heavy and thick, and her hair was soon twisting around her face, closing in on her vision and space to breathe.

With her breath running out and the Heerajras fighting her, Navas was close to losing this battle out in space. She was becoming weaker, and her blood darkened the waters furthermore. Her lungs were sore from constriction, her throat stabbed with pain, her neck was cut, and her bloodied legs had become weak from kicking the Heerajras away.

With one last push, she tried to shove a ravenous Heerajra away from her, its bare jaw snapping at her wildly. Its remaining eyeball was white and bloodied over, rattling in its socket, but its desperation was vivid. Navas felt a wave of blackness pass over her. The skull of the Heerajra, skinless, appeared from a cloud of her blood and hair, the concluding image in her life. A second before it all faded to black for her, she saw a purple light.

Navas was swiftly pulled from the waters, and she felt herself being hurled onto a hard surface. Spluttering to catch her breath, she coughed up brown particles and it took her a moment to realise she had been flung onto a little asteroid. She was far enough to see what had taken her in.

A giant cloud, resembling a slow-moving whale, floated through space, leaving rust-coloured particles in its wake. In its centre, Navas could see a Heerajra's skeletal hand reach out feebly towards the front of the cloud. That Heerajra must have owned a giant planet. She was grateful that hand didn't reach her in the cloud. As the cloud moved away, whatever was in its path was taken in and consumed, a gorging monster that spared nothing. Navas stared back, trying to make sense of what had happened and what she was looking at.

The cloud sparkled very dimly, the last throes of light and life trying to survive in the suffocating gas. Navas sat for a moment and almost cried. She was bone dry, but bleeding from her arms and mainly her neck. She had no idea where she was anymore and gripped the Queen's cape. The asteroid was not big enough for her to collapse on and she so wanted to rest.

To lie and catch her breath again. She felt like she needed to heave, to rid herself of the plasma, but the murky water left no trace on her, and the amount she coughed up had disappeared.

There isn't time to rest, she thought wearily.

Her family were being taken further and further away from her. She closed her eyes and pictured them all, one by one, trying to feel their energy, even Celd Dion's rage, or Goston's fear. Leifweiden's warmth.

Between her shaking, she felt nothing.

She had no sense of their energy near her at all. Sitting on a lone asteroid, she wondered how she'd even make it back home. She found the little rock that was in her cleavage and held it tightly. She gripped it in her fist and pressed her fist against her forehead. *This is real. This is home.* She shook from nerves. *My home.*

Her dress had become rags, a miniskirt with a single strip of her long skirt remaining, and sleeveless top, slipping away from her breasts. At least the cape remained, despite being stained red from her blood. Navas stood on the small asteroid and tried to reassure herself that it wasn't hopeless. She had to get back home with her family. She placed the precarious rock back down her sparse top.

If Liras were out here with her now, she'd not let Navas give up. She took a deep breath and shouted and shouted her sister's name. Loudly, she shouted her sister's nickname Lili, and strung out her name so that, in the end, she was yodelling her name out, badly. Navas laughed, half embarrassed, half relieved. She scooped up as much asteroid dust as she could and patted it down on the worst of her heavily bleeding wounds.

Celd Dion would hate that she was being silly, she realised, as she finished patching herself up. *I know this is serious, but I need to smile,* she said to him in her mind. *I want to keep going. To find you all.*
Even Iros, who was usually critical of her, would be appalled to see how battered she looked. Navas thought of Liras, who would be looking so bejewelled that there would barely be any space for the material of her dress to show through. Her family always thought she, Navas, looked dishevelled even when she was fully dressed. Navas smiled.
If only they could see her now. She let out a little scornful laugh. She wanted to meet everyone again, but this time in the same finery as Liras, she vowed. In no way could Leifweiden see her completely chewed up.

Navas floated up from the asteroid, bloodied, sooty and barely dressed, and began to travel in the opposite direction as the whale. Here, she felt the slightly warmer side of space. As she carried on, she was relieved to see the smudges of colours returning, the bright spiky stars. Even within the unstill gases there were specks of lights, twinkling like the stars back home.

She wondered what that purple light had been. Whatever it was, it had saved her.

Navas thought of the half-dead Heerajras and stopped for a moment. She knew she couldn't let her family become those who ate others. Those Heerajras had danced and felt something, happiness and anger, before they had become mindless beings. She hated to think that they had been in agony all this time. She wouldn't allow this for her family. With her resolve stronger, she quickened her pace, kicking her legs as hard as they could go, despite her energy levels nearing empty.

She wanted to try and find her family's energy again but had to make sure she was as far away from the whale cloud as possible. Those in the waters would confuse her feelings.

Navas felt far from home. She wondered if the Queen was safe. She swam past the soft lights and frozen gases that came back into view, and she wondered if her family had made it back somehow. Perhaps Geadeous had fought off The Quasar in her tyrant form and now they were all heading back.

She passed all of the wonderful spongy gases that appeared so fragile, yet were made of stone, like unfinished clay mountains. Navas smiled softly.

Princess Liras would wait on her green fields for so long for her. When she saw her sister, she'd run and hug her and hold her so tightly. They'd fall to the floor and Princess Liras would tell her the adventures she'd had, so joyfully. As Navas floated in the warmer, brightening space, stronger colours ever so slowly came back into view. Distant galaxies and strange lights, that were dim and didn't have the same sharpness as stars, began to fill her view.

Navas suddenly missed her easel. There would be so much for her to paint when she got back to her solar system. She stopped and grabbed an imaginary paintbrush and painted what she saw in front of her. The soft pastel gases, the hidden black and the many, *many* stars, all the Queens and Kings of their solar systems. Without the veil of her atmosphere, the stars were so plentiful, and their luminosity was strong, sharp icicles of light bursting from orbs of warmth.

The suns had families and homes and they all fought to survive the world around them.

Navas spun with her pretend paintbrush and finished her vision. She dragged her 'brush' to pull the pink through the black and feathered out the edges to soften the colour. A curve of her wrist completed a large star, and she flicked her hand to finish off the smattering of stars. This is what she'd show the others. She placed her hands on her hips and admired her canvas. The space around them seemed so distant and black from home but here, it was as colourful as a field of encompassing, shining tulips.

Navas grinned, then her smile faded, slowly. It was beautiful out here. She gently touched her neck. And savage.

Celd Dion would only scorn her for wasting time. She could hear his voice saying, "This isn't the time to be stargazing, girl!" Leifweiden would hold her from behind and say... she blushed and lowered her chin, a small smile playing on her lips.

Navas eventually came to a small planet, not so near that she could land, but enough to see the entire floating orb. She could see its sun far away, shining stronger than the other stars, and wondered if it was like Planet Entanerus.

She could land and visit the Heerajra. She could rest, say hello and they could help her on her journey. There wasn't a glass bridge here from what she could see. Navas reached the planet and closed her eyes. She couldn't sense any energy.

She frowned. Not a single trace of life and the planet itself was just a sphere. No weather, no water... no atmosphere. *How sad*, she thought. A planet is only as alive as its owner.

Floating on, Navas could hear the hum of electricity and hoped she was near anything, anyone, that would help her.

Bells rang out louder and, in the distance, galaxies were taking form as Navas watched.

These lights were not stars, but the remains of an attempt on their life. A galaxy came into focus, and she gasped slightly. Princess Liras had drawn in the sand what galaxies could look like, but this ghostly pale galaxy was being pulled by many black holes and now looked like a Heerajra hand. Soft piles of light and finger-shaped gases and knuckles were suspended in space as the black holes ate away.

The entire galaxy was reflected in her eye, and she stared in amazement. Navas knew the black holes were dangerous, but she could see the entire galaxy, and if she reached out, she felt as if they could make contact. An astral being and her, connecting in the meadow of stars and clouds. Navas floated towards it, past shadows of other distant dead planets. She was mesmerised by the galaxy hook.

She wasn't sure whether she was getting used to the scale in space, or if her mind was playing tricks on her. Reaching out, relieved to find a familiar shape, she smiled until she saw a bright purple light, on what would have been the index finger of the galaxy. She knew that if she got closer the galaxy would lose its shape, but she had a focal point now. Navas wanted it to be the same purple light that had saved her from the murky gas.

It looked far away, but she hadn't had the red particles to follow for a long while. She took a chance and went towards it, getting closer, the hand now dissipating.

Navas saw that it was a purple star threaded with spaghetti twirls and wafts of light, moving more like seaweed underwater rather than the fiery rain looping over The Sun. The hairs on her arms stood up the closer she got, when she realised the star wasn't large at all. Its light swirled far beyond its surface, long wreaths of energy making a perfect shield around its small being.

Navas decided not to get any closer. Its energy was something she had never felt before. This purple light had saved her, but it felt incredibly hostile. As she turned, she felt dizzy and passed out.

The Magnetar

Navas fluttered her heavy eyes to see very polished shoes and long, purple-suited legs. She screamed and found herself in front of the Heerajra who owned the purple star. Her surroundings were nothing but purple light, and she floated on a flat rock in front of the Heerajra's star as he looked down happily. She had gotten so close to the galaxy that she assumed (incorrectly) she was now in it.

Floating gently around her were flat-topped rocks. Their surfaces were so clean and unblemished that they reflected each light pixel, making them glow like purple lamps.

Navas coughed and sputtered and couldn't understand how she had got to this point. She saw nothing but the purple light.

The space around her was all shades of purple, melting and dipping into black and then lilac, to mauve and to purple indigo. In front of her was a man in a long-tailed coat, with a purple marbled walking stick and a gold mask that covered his eyes and cheeks. He wore a top hat over his flicky, long purple hair and seemed at ease in the twisting and merging psychedelic world. The Heerajra used the glowing, flat rocks as stepping stones.

"Where am I?" Navas asked, noticing her dress was even more badly torn. Her body ached from fatigue and bruises.

"Hello, little mess? This is my Magnetar."

"My name is Navas. Not 'little mess'," she replied haughtily. "What's yours? What was that water cloud? It was your light, wasn't it? I saw it in there?" Navas placed her hand on her chest, feeling so weak and breathless.

"So many…questions," said the Heerajra deliberately. "You can call me…" He looked down briefly and shrugged as he said, "Remanence. That will do for now. It drowns anything that comes into contact with it. It slowly kills them, unlike… a black hole that obliterates stars. It chokes all beings, slowly, carefully. You're a planet – what are you doing all the way out here?"

"I'm looking for a Quasar." Navas sat and covered herself, feeling completely bare.

Remanence shook his head. Navas struggled to breathe normally, her lungs feeling as though a rock was slowly being pressed down onto her chest.

"The Quasar has been very…ah, foolish," frowned Remanence. "Why has he reached out to you? Better still, why are you looking for him?" Navas picked up that he would speak rapidly or slowly, as if he had forgotten how to say particular words.

"He's taken all my friends." Navas stood up slowly on the little rock and took a deep, painful breath in. She was sweating and wanted nothing more than to jump into her oceans at home. *How long do I have? I'm falling apart*, were her very quiet thoughts.

"I can't stop," she continued. "Have you seen him? He's a man, black hair... red suit. All this space, and no one has seen him." Each breath she took felt like fire, and her voice took a hardened edge.

The man shook his head. "I can try and find him, but I'm not sure what energy signals he has. It would be…the word…tremendous, but there would be so many bodies he's taken…" He looked at his staff. "I think they can hush their energy far…faster than we can," he added. "It's amazing, isn't it? A giant monster can hide from all our stars."

Remanence turned to go back to his star, the purple star that had twirling and molten flares sprouting from its shell. Navas was far more used to yellow light. As the man moved to go back to his Kassel, he skittered on the flat rocks.

Navas decided to ignore the man's compliments towards The Quasar.

"I've never seen a purple star before. A yellow and blue…" she saw a flash of the white room and winced. "It's nicer. Do you have a home?" She couldn't imagine there being a building on the small star.

Remanence stopped to answer her. "A Kassel? Well, I call it, ah, home. It's a power plant. It's like a puzzle, this star. It holds so much power, yet all…hidden in its core." He grinned. "Perhaps like you, little mess."

Remanence knew Navas needed to rest and the metal in her voice sounded like she was getting irritable, but the energy from his star was far too strong for her. She'd surely fold in half if she went inside. He wondered what to give her to help, but saw her pupils dilate, her irises so thin they looked like gold rings.

As Navas watched the Heerajra in front of her, she felt a drag in her stomach and could feel her arms growing numb. Remanence was talking to her, and she narrowed her eyes. Her vision was becoming unfocused, and the high squeal of feedback pierced through her ears. All she could hear was a fuzzy deep voice as his mouth moved.

The Magnetar and Remanence pixelated and became distorted in front of her, glitching and ghosting. Navas covered her eyes and tried to look at him again, but he was getting blurrier and blurrier by the second. The purple skies and floors became kaleidoscopic and, with the blurring and glitching, became a purple horror. The lightest purples shone almost white, skirting from becoming true white, and the darkest, deepest purples never falling into the colour black.

Her nose began to bleed, and she covered her ears to block out the stuttering, screeching sound. Her hands went to her stomach, nausea rising as lightest-purple and black-purple mandalas appeared dancing in front of her,

Remanence and The Magnetar both being swallowed up by the jarring, liquid colours. Navas could no longer feel the rock beneath her, and a heavy synthesised note began to compress each one of her cells.

Every passing line of colour throbbed and rippled, terrifying her. Every which way she looked were more bands of flashing and falling colours, with sounds of squealing feedback, heavy droning notes and a blipping that incessantly rapped over all of these awful sounds. Suddenly, Navas felt the Remanence's mask being placed on her face and everything restored itself, so instant, that a wave of pain flashed through her skull.

"What was that?" she panted, touching the gold mask with her fingertips. On the rock, she became very limp, her head almost in her lap.
In that instance of Remanence's mask touching her, everything was back to normal. He had revealed his face. His eyes were balls of plasma, his light purple skin scarred with veins, etched by purple fire. The sclera of his eyes were pitch black and his irises ebbed with veins of electricity.

"My energy is a little too much," he said gently. "I'm trying to contain it, but I cannot for long. I don't have too much, ah, control anymore. The mask can help you use my energy. It used to be an entire suit, but this is all that remains. What do you think? I look better in purple, no?" He held out his arms to show off his suit, a dazzling smile on show.

Navas smiled wearily back. His eyes... they barely looked like eyes... they looked so painful.

"Will you be ok here? Without it?" she asked.

The man laughed and lowered his top hat. "I am of this energy. Let me search for him. I will return shortly."

"Can I rest?" asked Navas. Her leg and neck, she realised, were still bleeding. "I just want to go home."

"You're as near to my home as you can be," replied the man. "I know you want to rest. You want to lie down. Ah, sleep, even." He said the words carefully.

Remanence had lost his ability to search out other stars naturally, but could do so in his home, the power plant, where millions of monitors showed images around the space he was in. He made his way to the monitor room, where dials and levers controlled the cameras. All he had in his home was beaten-up furniture and a hat stand. He removed his jacket and placed it on the stand, to reveal a very light lilac shirt. He rolled up his sleeves. The metal around him was the darkest purple and all of his other rooms and buildings had long gone, absorbed into the fires of his star. Occasionally, he could hear the deep creak and clang of metal, the old sounds of a factory. Remanence pressed some buttons on his console and the static of the screens switched from white to black to fuzzy images of the world around him. He stabbed his walking stick into a port and closed his eyes as his palms embraced the black orb.

    Navas waited and looked up at the small star. Around her, she could see faint stars in the distance, opaque purple light obscuring their view, and was glad she was not in the purple mess anymore. She was floating still on the rock and gently touched the mask. As she stared out, her eyes became unfocused. For a moment, her mind was completely thoughtless. It rarely happened to her, but she felt she could stare forever, for miles.

Remanence used his stick to tap her on the shoulder from behind and she jumped.

"Go here, planet." He held his stick out and pointed with it into space, away from his star.

"Thank you." Navas looked hesitant and Remanence asked if she wanted him to join her.

"No. I can do this." She stood up unsteadily. "I'm just… tired."

"I will be able to find my mask," said Remanence. "I am always connected to it. Act, ah, with haste. Use it to get back here. You are far from your home, aren't you?"

She nodded. She thought of her easel and grassy plains. And tea, too. When was the last time she held her mug?

"Thank you, you are so kind."

"Kind…yes," echoed Remanence. "But is there anything you can do for me?"

Navas looked about her and shook her head. "I have nothing." She took off the mask.

Remanence placed his hand over her heart, his fingertips pressing hard into Glaruntia's golden, bloodied cape.

"This, ah, cape... let me have it as a reminder of you. I can wrap it around my staff." His eyes widened, the electricity sputtering out from the sockets.

She nodded and reluctantly took the cape off. She hated being so bare, but she needed his help.

"It's so soft, this...cape," murmured Remanence. "From your star, no? I used to be golden. You wouldn't be so afraid of me if I was."

Navas looked down. "I'm not afraid—"

Remanence leant in close to her face, his scars more visible and deeper than she realised. Electricity pulsed through his veins, and his eyes were ebbing with a bright current. They looked like miniature suns, with long webs of light spanning from the centre.

"I am not afraid." Navas replied with as much conviction as she could. She wondered how he would look when he was gone. Would their Queen become this in another life? Thinking of Polymir, and his recent form, she smiled at Remanence and placed a hand on his cheek. She felt a massive shock and her hand snapped back. Remanence laughed, and she placed the mask on and tried again.

Navas smirked. "See? I'm not afraid."

As soon as she said this, the star rippled and, within seconds, a burst of energy erupted from its north pole, a splutter of purple light energy. For a second, the magnetic field of the entire star was illuminated so that it was encased in a bright, electrifying cage.

To protect her, Remanence embraced Navas, his hand on the back of her head so that she could just see over his shoulder. For a long while, it felt like she had forgotten how to blink, her heart pounding fast.

He closed his eyes, the purple light pushing through his eyelids, not having felt a touch for many years.

"This feels... nice?" sighed Remanence. "That word... Go, Heerajra. No star eater shall have the satisfaction of taking moons as well."

Navas could feel her energy leaving her. All she wanted to do was sleep now. She didn't know how much longer she could go on for. Or how she had lasted this long. Regardless of who it was, to be held was all she needed at this point.

"Why... why are you helping me?" she had to ask him, her voice fatigued.

Very slowly, Remanence released her and tapped his nose. "No, it's nothing. But, seeing you reminded me of someone. A ghost now. But I don't have much time, so I can do as much, ah, good as I can." He turned back to look at his star. "I wish... we could have more fun."

Navas felt a pang. She agreed with him. She just wanted to be silly. She wanted to paint, to play in the oceans, or even drink with Iros. Her leg was slick with blood. Her neck felt so fragile. She wanted tea, as well. She *needed* tea.

"When I return, we can," she replied gently. "My sister would love to meet you."

Remanence nodded, not turning back to look at her. Navas had to quickly diminish the thought of hugging him again. She had to keep going.

"I'd like to meet her. Your family." Remanence turned to her and grinned. "If they're as, ah, entertaining as you." As light as a feather, he hopped and skipped back to his home. Navas couldn't imagine so much space inside such a small star. She would have to convince him to let her and the others in when she got back.

The Reunion

Navas had her resolve restored. She would get her family and friends back. The Quasar may eat her alive, burn or pierce her, but she needed to try.

She kept the mask in her firm grip. *I'm on my way, Liras*, she thought. She looked back at The Magnetar and could see giant loops of the magnetic field singing with energy. *What a beautiful, strange star*, she thought. The loops looked bigger than the star itself.

The mask, she realised, left such strong light beams as it moved with her, it looked like a lit-up handrail behind her.

On a monitor screen, Remanence watched as Navas flew on, with the purple light from his mask trailing behind her. He looked at his gloved palm and closed his eyes. *Surely, I had a solar system? A family, too? A real name?* He clenched his fist, trying to remember, images and memories of long ago appearing and disappearing, brief stills of a time long ago. He opened his eyes and saw nothing. All he had to think about was the little

Heerajra, knowing it was his duty as a sun... a bygone sun... to look out for their solar system.

"Onward, little planet. Victory will be yours," he said quietly to the empty room.

Navas was terrified. The mask conveyed her rapidly through space, and in her grip, it felt hot to the touch. She now had a road to follow, a path. It should have been completely reassuring for her, but what if Remanence had lied to her? What if stars, who were no longer a king or queen, became dangerous? She wished Leifweiden was here. His voice was a balm to her worries. She wanted to trust Remanence. As an old King, he must have been an honourable man... She was running out of options. As she jetted through the cold world, she saw a curtain of light and sparkling crystals ahead of her. It was as tall as her current self, being as large as Planet Navas, and it went on for miles, either side of her.

She came to a stop before the icy, misty screen, the gems bouncing with light as she did so. She reached out and touched a diamond that was the size of her fist.

Navas looked to the left and right of her but couldn't tell what had left this beautiful trail. She slowly moved through it and gasped. It was so cold, but so incredibly rejuvenating, taking her breath away for a second. She laughed and felt goosebumps all over her body as she shivered. She turned around to face the diamonds and felt tears in her eyes. She would take everyone back here, she decided. Leifweiden, with all his stargazing, would have been besotted with what was out here in this space.

She looked down at the mask in her hand and realised it wasn't burning anymore. Moving further away, the ice wall now behind her, she saw in the distance a giant comet chugging along the world, spewing the icy white materials away from it. It was the same size as her yet left such a large effervescent veil. Navas felt so tranquil, watching the comet leave her view. The comet was losing its surface, and yet carried on with its journey. The azure comet lit up like flame, yet it was so cold at its nucleus. As much as it was lost, and slowly being taken away, Navas found it serene to watch.

As she savoured watching the comet's solitary journey, a little red pixel interrupted her view. She blinked in surprise. Was this actually in front of her?

She reached out and cradled the pixel loosely between her hands. She let it go and it quivered like a fleeing butterfly, and she followed it. The minute spark would lead her to him, and all her family. She took a deep breath and followed her new, tiny guide. He was so close again, closer than he had been for so long. Thanks to Remanence, she would find her family. The red glitter eventually led her to a pink gateway, its appearance slowly becoming stronger against the blackness of space and stars. It looked like a pink-walled maze, suspended without the aid of a planet's purpose. As Navas entered through the gates, everything became pink, in different shades and depths, and the smell of perfume filled the air. She felt like she was in a floral bath floating on a pink cloud.

She realised she hadn't smelt anything in for so long. The salty waters at home, a flower on newly rained soil. Even the malodorous smell of the volcanoes, of mud fire and chemicals.

She stepped hesitantly through the first archway and floated on. Each brick was large and soft, as cushiony as candy floss. Each tunnel led to a soft brick wall. Each tunnel that she went down, left and right, led to a brick wall. Navas couldn't afford to get lost. She dug her fingernails into the walls and, over a short time, the finger grooves vanished so she had to move on quickly. There was a ceiling to the tunnels, which meant she couldn't determine an exit overhead.

How could The Quasar be here? How could it fit in here, in this maze? Could the mask help her here, like it did with the corruption she felt near the purple star? The fragrance was making her swoon. How she wanted to be home now. As time went on, she was no nearer to the centre of the maze, and she became frustrated. She tried to go through the walls, but to no avail. Confusingly, the cushiony walls were impenetrable.

Navas closed her eyes tightly and tried to sense The Quasarjra. Nothing. There wasn't any energy here. She shoved on the mask and, for the briefest second, the walls became black, webbed with purple strands of energy.

She saw the Heerajras standing in front of her, her family, but they were washed out, as if she was looking through a drenched window.

They disappeared as quickly as they came. Her heart skipped a beat. With the mask, she followed the images of her family, the watery defocused images of them. She felt like she was suspended only by the thin purple strands, the soft pink walls now stripped of flesh, only their nerves remaining. She didn't have time to be repulsed.

Navas soon found herself on a path leading to the centre of the maze. As she moved deeper into the maze, she could hear a faint song being played, creaking and off-key. Navas had no idea it was Liras's song for the Queen.

***

Glaruntia, far back in space where Navas lived, had barely any home left. Sitting down next to a sinking statue, she closed her eyes and faced up to the sky above her. Where was her daughter? Glaruntia wanted to see her family's faces, and clasped her hands together, fretfully. She'd compressed her energy all this time in case they were due back soon. *There is no need to restrain,* she thought hazily.

She stood up, her cape floating like a rising tsunami behind her. Bells began to clang, and her entire star began to sing and sizzle, the heat increasing swiftly. The colours of the rainbow flashed through her irises, her hair blew wildly, and a storm of fire raged over the surface of The Sun. Rainbows, in massive arcs, looped over the entire Sun.

However, Glaruntia, such was her focus, didn't realise they were appearing. All she could think of was her family and her anger towards The Quasar.

Sounds and energy warped and collided with each other, discordant noises wrapping with the trembling light. Finally releasing her anger, Glaruntia took her energy to such a height, that the first shell of her sun's energy escaped outwards into the solar system and beyond, the blast of the wind rattling even the planets, with a green wave of light chasing after it.

The golden, melting city rippled and glittered with crackling sparks of energy. The light and heat of her outburst dissipated slowly, but her Sun glowed brighter than ever, despite this, filling the solar system with a vibrant energy. Glaruntia was at full strength now, her desperation to find her daughter a physical need. How much longer could Navas remain out there, in the absolute of space?

Panting slightly, Glaruntia turned as another statue fell into the pool of liquid gold. She sat and floated above the destruction. Her star was so strong now, yet it was dying, the expense of energy fuelling its deep fires stronger than ever before.
Glaruntia floated to the top of a sinking skyscraper for safety and tried to quieten the star's fires, so that her family could at least be near her. The outburst of heat and crackle dissipated slowly into the atmosphere.
More and more buildings were dragged into the fiery oceans and, no matter how hard she focused to calm her energy, her star was now too hot.

***

As Navas snaked through the maze, the iron ring that Glaruntia had given her began to glow slightly green. However, she hadn't yet noticed.

In the centre of the pink maze, Navas found herself in a large square space, walled by pink petals.

She saw a large, coffin-shaped bed surrounded by pink nicotiana flowers, mixed with Four O'Clocks of a deeper shade of pink. The flowers were in a canopy that hung from a hoop, with lace draping and trailing over the large bed. Small sequins sparkled over the drapes and shone pink, to match the surroundings. At any other time, it would have been beautiful.

Red and purple variants of the flowers were surrounding the coffin and Navas could see a figure in the bed. She took the mask off, ignoring the prickly sensation it left on her skin.

As she crept closer to the bed, she realised the maze was absurdly silent.

As Navas crept even closer, she saw that the figure in the bed was Princess Liras. Navas gasped but felt breathless at the same time.

Navas stood over the bed and had an image of Princess Liras as a baby, bawling in her crib on The Moon. Navas saw that her sister's face was pale, whiter than pearl. It was cratered, broken, with scars all over her cheeks, her eyes caving into the sockets. Her usually blush lips were a deep purple. Liras was covered in flowers, and her hands were clasped over her chest, a flower threaded through her fingertips. Her hair was down, its metallic sheen lost. Navas touched her sister's cheek very carefully, and it was cold enough to make Navas retract her hand.

Oh, just be asleep, she pleaded.

Navas looked around to see if there were any other coffins or beds, but there was nothing else but Princess Liras's shrine. Navas wanted to sit with Liras, but the bed was completely brimming with the small flowers, so there was no room. She knelt by the bed and touched Princess Liras's hand gently.

It was a strange feeling, seeing Princess Liras here. Navas hadn't known what to expect when she eventually saw her sister again. She reasoned the same, mad, red

Quasarjra had her tied up. Or had chained her. But alive. Always alive… she frowned.

Liras herself had once imparted the Queen's knowledge on life cycles. Navas remembered how Liras used the tulips dying back home as an example, how they grew and wilted. How stars grew from space and how they could end in a celebration of fire or… become black holes. Become monsters.

So far removed from their gentle nature. Navas began to cry, her tears falling freely down her face.

"I love you, sister," she sobbed.

"I loved her too."

Navas spun around to see The Quasarjra behind her, and quickly stood up.

"What is this?" she hissed.

The Quasarjra smiled. He was taller than Navas remembered. He was still at a relative height to her, but he had looked shorter when he was in front of his chariot. He'd definitely looked less imposing.

"You have come a long way, little planet," he derided. "You look like you have been eaten up and spat out."

His feline eyes narrowed more. "How did you find us?"

"Us... the others, where are they?" asked Navas, her voice hollow. "Leifweiden and Geadeous? My family, where are they?"

The Quasarjra frowned. "The others? They were eaten that time I saw you all. Except for their planets."

Navas staggered and fell to the floor. She took a deep breath in, shaking, desperate not to cry in front of The Quasarjra. He spoke so simply; she couldn't be sure she had even asked the question properly.

"If I took everything," he continued, "Princess Liras would have been upset. I had to give her hope. That she could visit her family one day."

Navas backed onto the bed, her eyes focused on a flower ahead of her. "*You* killed them all." She could feel her heart become colder.

"Not the Princess."

Navas nodded absently. "She died being so close to you for so long, didn't she?"

She looked at the mask in her hand.

"She didn't die because of me—" began The Quasarjra.

Navas glared at him. "You killed my entire family. There was nothing left for Princess Liras to see at home.

Tell me, did she speak to you? Did she cry? Did she smile at all?" Tears were falling unrestrained from her eyes now.

The Quasarjra flashed his teeth as he smiled, an irritatingly dashing smile.

"Those are my memories now." He walked to the coffin and leant over Princess Liras. Navas quickly stood up, as if to stop him from going any nearer. He very carefully moved one strand of hair away from Princess Liras's face. Just as he was about to lean in to kiss her, Navas grabbed his wrist and pushed it back.

"Don't touch her! You can't anymore. I'm taking her home."

The Quasarjra rubbed his wrist and laughed tartly. After sweeping his eyes over Liras, he folded his arms and cocked his head. "How? How can you get back? Do you even know where you are? How far are you from the little sun?"

Navas shook her head determinedly. The action made her gasp from the pain in her neck.

"I don't care," she replied, her voice breaking. "Even if I can't get back, I want her out of here. Even if we both freeze, or burn, even if we're out there forever." She gestured angrily away from the coffin. "She'll be away from you!" She gripped the mask harder. "It wasn't worth it, was it?"

The Quasarjra picked a purple Four O'Clock. "No, little planet. The time I had with her was *all* worth it." Navas felt her heart pulling apart slowly, as if each word he spoke was unthreading her very sinews.
She looked at Princess Liras, whose face resembled a broken porcelain doll. Her sister used to smile, laugh and blush. Her sister used to feel and move. She'd worry about her hair, clothes and marvel. Marvel at the world around her. Marvel over a tulip… She cared about her family, the future and she made everyone happy. Her Queen, her guidepost, was her love. A caring being.

Navas glowered at The Quasarjra, who still gazed at Princess Liras with complete adoration. There wasn't any way these two could have been together, as his energy was too much. Just like she couldn't stay in the blue star, or in The Magnetar. Even if Liras *had* chosen to be with this monster, it would have been impossible. He seemed to read her mind.

"I must unleash soon," he said. "I feel like I'm holding my breath for both of you."

"How do you think you could have been a partner for my sister?" Navas didn't even know why she asked this.

"She loved her family, didn't she?" he replied. "Haven't you looked across the skies and been transfixed by a light? By a spark, a colour or a world? And haven't you ever wondered what it is? As I got closer, I could see just how beautiful she was. She called for me."

Navas shook her head angrily, her neck singing with pain. "We *hated* your red light."

How she wished Leifweiden was here. Her throat was in agony from crying and from the Heerajra attack. Leifweiden was hurt, last she remembered. There was blood…

"I've watched her grow up," sustained The Quasarjra. "To become a woman. Such a beautiful white light."

Navas's eyes widened. She didn't think her heart could hurt anymore. Her throat felt thick, and she was still bleeding from her neck. Her leg was bleeding. His words seemed to hurt so much more than her physical wounds. She pressed the mask between her fingers.

She couldn't let him hurt anyone else, from this moment on. What if he chased another moon, star or planet? What if someone else's sister got hurt?

The mask was all she had in her arsenal. There was a chance she could fuel his energy. There was a chance he could be depleted of it.

Navas turned back to her sister and, with a featherlight touch, placed her hands on hers. She inhaled deeply and released her breath, slowly, wanting her emotions to be exhaled as well.

"You're taking up my time, planet. I'm getting bored," The Quasarjra said stonily, as he ran his pale hand through his immaculate hair.

Swallowing hard, she said to him, "Unleash the Quasar. Show me the power you had when you took my family. My friends. My heart." Her voice broke as she said this.

"Why?" he laughed arrogantly. "Why would I do that for you?"

Navas had to keep her voice strong. She looked down at her mauled sister, then walked up close to The Quasarjra, so that she was inches away from him.

"If I can't take her, then I want to be with her."
He smirked and placed his hand on his red tie pin. He backed off from Navas and went to Liras, kissing her lips gently.

Standing as far back as he could from Liras, The Quasarjra pressed his tie pin and unleashed his power. The accretion disc burst from behind him, immediately filling up the space around both him and Navas.
The red light seeped into every corner and the blowtorch noise crashed around Navas's ears. Flowers and petals flew away from the square and all that was left was the coffin and Liras. She looked so defenceless. Navas winced and craned her neck, to see how big The Quasar actually was. It was impossible. She needed to be miles and miles away. The pink fog dissipated until they were surrounded by red and the black of space, the depth of The Void seeping through now. Loose petals spun wildly around them both, like a pink flurry of snow.
"Thank you for showing me this," Navas said, her voice unaffected by the roar of the accretion disc. She stepped closer to The Quasarjra, who backed off, thinking she was going to kiss him.

"Give me back my sister, monster."

He shook his head, unsmiling. He wasn't on his steps anymore. There were only inches between them now. Navas had a second to look into his ruby coloured eyes that held nothing but malice in them.

His eyes seemed to light up as he scowled at her, as did the disc behind him. The red light surrounding them made Navas think of the sunsets at home and how The Sun used to warm her studio. But this wasn't home. This wasn't sunlight, but the energy of destroyed beings.
"Let her be my reminder of lost love, my beautiful, painful reminder." As The Quasarjra spoke, the accretion disc rippled and spiked with his sound waves.
"You *forced* your love on her!" shouted Navas.
"I couldn't hurt you, or your sun, when she was alive." He materialised a red whip in his hands. The Quasarjra snapped it around Navas's neck and began to choke her. "But now she's not here to stop me!"
He flung his arm out so that Navas fell to the floor and the mask dropped out of her hand. Just as she tried to reach for the mask, The Quasarjra used more whips to thwack her on her back, making her scream out.

Navas tried to reach for the mask again, but The Quasarjra grabbed her by her white hair and yanked her back, then twisted the strands around his palm into a tight fist. Trying to escape, Navas pulled as hard as she could and one of his whips singed her hair off. She fell forwards, her hair shorn off to her nape. With escape in sight, she tried once more to reach for the mask as she heard the crack of the whip. She was so close; she couldn't give up! Between her shaking, reaching fingertips, she felt the mask.

Navas felt her neck burn and, for a second, thought the whip would tear through her neck. She fell to her hands and knees and pulled as hard as she could, the whip as taut as a guitar string. As she pulled and pulled, more whips were wrapping around her ankles and wrists. Her free hand was being wrenched backwards and her legs were being lifted from the floor. With her last ounce of strength, and a mighty yell, she clutched the mask and hastily slapped it onto her face, her arm rebounding from the whip's unyielding grip.

A pulse left the mask, a purple light. Then, like ink seeping into paper, the purple light travelled up the red whip.

The Quasarjra watched in confusion as the red light was being eaten away. The purple light left the mask, sucking up through the red whips around Navas's wrists and neck, and rapidly to The Quasarjra himself. Soon, the blowtorch noise became erratic, and the accretion disc began to tick wildly, but in a heavier, mechanical way. In an aid to stop the purple light drenching him, Navas was released from the cords, and she gasped for breath on the floor. The Quasarjra's face was stricken.
"What have you done?" he bellowed. Angrily, he clenched his fists, the red energy now fighting the purple back from the disc and himself. His eyes became so red and lit up that they emitted light, his irises flaring as bright as his accretion disc.
In his rage, The Quasarjra materialised a single blade in his right hand. As the two energies fought for dominance, the purple eating away at the red, and the red

desperately trying to fight it back, he crashed the sword down on Navas.

However, a green flash of light surged out from her, stopping the blade before it reached her forearm. In the same flash of light, Navas was now wearing an Anarkali dress, an emerald-green silk frock that covered her arms, stomach and legs as the material raced down to her ankles. A deep sea blue chunni looped over her shoulder. She couldn't feel the gold jewellery materialise over her, bangles, a tika and earrings. Each metal piece, pressed in with aqua zircons. Navas had no idea in this havoc, her clothes had changed to something Liras would adore her in.

The Quasarjra could feel the acidic burn of the purple light over his skin and now, in his fury, used both hands to thunder the blade on her. Each blade strike hit a green force shield that protected Navas, as she feebly used her forearms to protect herself from the weapon.

The Quasarjra went from rage to confusion, the blade above his head like a beacon.

"What is your star doing here? Where is her planet?" he growled.

Her Majesty? Navas thought suddenly.

Navas could feel the Queen's energy, too, in this chaos of flying petals, noise and lights.

The Quasarjra was shuddering from the toxic Magnetar light eating at him, but his rage seemed to fight back as best it could. The accretion disc was still a bone-aching jet engine of noise, but all she needed was her arm to protect her from the blade. Navas tried to scramble away, but The Quasarjra materialised another sword and hurled it before her, blocking her path.

He laughed bitterly.

"The Queen followed you here? Or are you now the Queen? You're wearing her crown of light and aura."

His voice was mocking.

Navas had no idea what he was talking about but reached up to her head. She could feel it now. The warmth of their Sun.

The iron ring, nestled with her haath phool, glowed a soft, dancing green aura and, for a moment, she laughed with relief. Only now did she notice her clothes had changed. *My Majesty...*

She stood up and shook her head in determination.

"You can't hurt me!" she cried out happily. "You can't hurt us anymore! My Queen is protecting me!"

The Quasarjra rapidly calculated all that he could to break through the green shield and, despite the purple light eroding at his red, the effect of the purple and red light a hallucinogenic horror, he fired more bands of fizzing energy at Navas, but they all slapped off of her. Frantically, he pushed so much energy at her that, in the end, he couldn't see her through the red light.

As the light of his desperate energy dimmed, Navas still stood, and now it was her turn to smirk at him, through his barrage of red whips that felt featherlight now.

As Navas approached him, he tried to use his fists to knock her and her shield down, but each punch bounced off the shield's surface.

He even tried to pull the shield away from her, his fingertips gripping into the shield's soft light, which was as hard as diamond.

Navas's face softened as she reached him.

"I can't let you hurt anyone else anymore."

The Quasarjra roared in her face, the accretion disc roaring behind him as he did so.

Calmly, Navas placed The Magnetar's mask on his face, a blast of purple light bursting from the contact as she did so. The Quasarjra tried to push the purple light away as it ate away his red light and his suit became purple. With an eruption of screams and cries, the accretion disc became completely purple, the red finally losing its battle.

Each light, one by one, dimmed out, each pixel and particle being consumed by The Magnetar's purple light. The Quasarjra tried to release another cord to inflict pain on Navas, but it fell from him, like a ribbon, and merely brushed past the shield.

  In a last grasp of effort, he tried to create steps to reach into the mouth of the portal, but they shattered instantly. Trying to pull the mask off from his face, The Quasarjra screamed in agony, doubling over as the purple light masticated his being.

Navas rushed to her sister's side. She could feel her wrists and neck burning from the pain and hoped it wasn't the same energy that tore through Geadeous. There was so much blood, already drenching her new dress.

Navas felt faint.

The Quasarjra, now in a heap, looked up at his once searingly red disc and the entire disc shuddered and screamed as he did so. His sparkling red eyes became a muted lavender and unfocused, like his body and mind, which were no longer working together. At the centre of his disc, a white light tried to fight against the magnetic acid of the purple light.

Navas shielded herself from the outstanding white light with her arm and pressed her forearm of her other arm over one ear. The light was so bright, she didn't think her eyes could even comprehend it. It was too much.

Despite the loss of the red light and the purple rapidly taking over, The Quasarjra swivelled his eyes to take one last look at Princess Liras.

The Quasarjra's final roar descended, and he went from a twenty-something man to a middle-aged man to an old man, until he became a skeleton. From purple, the entire disc became a deep green-brown colour in a ripple and

The Quasarjra crumbled away, leaving the mask to float freely.

The entire body of gas and light soon dimmed so that there was not a single spark left. Very slowly, like a giant moving to stand up, the portal began to float away from Navas.

She watched until she had a clear view and was surprised to see it looked skull-like, with deep black eye sockets and a slack mouth. The silence washed over her like a wave, such a contrast from the ticking and jet-engine scream of The Quasar. The skull would float amongst the other gloomy clouds and gaseous mountains in The Void forever.

Navas wondered if her family could be reborn from all of this. Did they know she was there? Could they see all that had happened? Had they been eaten? She closed her eyes lightly, the mask suspended in the air. She reached to take it down, and, as she did this, she saw the green aura leave her iron ring, her clothes returning to their original state. She watched in rumination as the emerald-green silk and jewels faded into a whisper of green light.

The Quasar was now gone, and it could no longer hurt other planets or moons. Navas felt her neck had been severely burnt. Her skin was burnt, close enough to splitting, yet The Quasarjra hadn't been using his full power. He must have wanted Liras to be semi-protected all this time. She looked at her hands.
If she looked very closely, she could see tiny pinpricks of blood. Shakily, she very slowly placed the mask on her face.

She went to sit with Princess Liras and then picked her up, awkwardly. Her embellished dress made her even heavier. Although Navas didn't walk on a surface, she still had to use her energy to move, and she was exhausted.

She took one more look at the dead Quasar, just to make sure it hadn't moved or showed any trace of coming back to life. It clung in the air, along with the lives of so many he had eaten, a motif of what he had done to so many lives and homes.

Navas realised she hadn't held Princess Liras in her arms since she was a baby. Navas smiled slightly. "Let's go home, sister."

The Queen

It was awkward holding her sister and she was so tired. She made it back to The Magnetar, the mask and Remanence's energy connection strong, and placed her sister in front of the man on the floating rock as he took his mask back. Navas bowed her head in sadness and, before she was affected by the magnet's energy, she thanked Remanence and went to pick up Princess Liras to continue her journey back home.
"How do I get home?" she asked wearily.
"Where is this, ah, Quasar?" he asked. "What happened to your beautiful hair?"
"It's hollow. He's gone now. So is my hair. Your mask... destroyed him."
Remanence nodded thoughtfully. He wasn't even sure he was capable of destroying anything. Bittersweet, he had helped this little planet, but his energy was completely corruptive. He was glad; however, he could still lend her his help.

She looked so beaten. He wished he was warmer and could let her rest a while; but each moment she was here, she was getting hurt.

"Can you get me home?" she asked.

"I cannot tell where you are from…," said Remanence.

"Is there anything you own from the planet you are from?"

Navas reached for her pouch, but it was burnt. The pebble she kept was dead energy.

"My sister and I are of our homes."

"I need, ah, an object."

She closed her eyes tightly. "The cape... and this!" She placed Princess Liras down gently and was about to take off her iron ring, but Remanence took her cape off of his staff and placed the gold material over his hand.

He ventured back to his monitors in his factory and Navas breathed in and out slowly, resisting holding her breath until he came out. After a while he returned, cape in hand.

"Here. It's so faint but feels so warm. It's towards that direction."

He watched as Navas lifted Princess Liras and she managed to bow to him, his wonderful purple star burning behind him.

"Thank you. I can finally go home." She tried not to cry or pass out. She had a question to ask him. "How do the stars see it all?"

"It's ah…our energy," he replied. "We can…could…feel the waves of the space around us. Do one thing for me. Be at peace. You have ah, accomplished a great feat." She smiled sadly. Remanence slowly tore off more of Navas's skirt and wrapped the piece of fabric over Princess Liras's closed eyes.

"I should see you again," cracked Navas. "I can bring my Queen back and—"

"I may not be here," replied Remanence. "The star killer is gone, and I am ah, happy. I hope your queen has peace, also." He frowned slightly as his mind tried to recall another memory, another word, another feeling. Navas smiled and could feel the tears on her face. "I'm sure you had a wonderful home. Your planets and stars." Her wrists suddenly pricked with pain.

Remanence laughed. "I'm sure I did. Maybe I had my own princess..." He knitted his brow, wishing he could remember. "Ah. Planet. Onwards, now. If you get lost, I'll try to help."

Navas continued back home, and she wondered if her own Sun would change colour one day. Blue, purple, the colours all seemed so unusual to her.

Remanence looked down at the gold, bloodied material of the cape and wrapped it over his staff and smiled.

He ventured back to his home, the power plant. *My planets*, he thought hazily. *My family.* He sat down on the rickety chair in front of a monitor and watched Navas fly home. *What a pretty name*, he thought. *I had a family, didn't I?* He closed his eyes for a moment. The screens flickered. *Try to remember, maybe.* He opened his eyes and looked down at his hands, his veins purple. *I hope I'll remember you, Navas.* He took the gold cape and held it between his hands. *Gold...*

A monitor screen fizzled with static and went black.

Navas wished that Princess Liras was awake so that she could see the world around her. She had to pause and wipe her tears away and her sister was heavy. She wanted to stop off at a planet, but she didn't know if the inhabitants were dangerous. She felt she had been gone for a long time. She had no setting sun to tell how many days, weeks or years she was gone. Each planet and star had its own timescales, its own day spans and orbits. She felt stronger, at least with purpose, following the red trail of The Quasar.

But now, the thought of turning up to see the Queen, figuratively empty-handed, made her ache.

She wished everyone was here. She wished that everyone was behind her, laughing and in awe at the sights outside of their home. Goston, accepting how brave she could be, how she could face her fears, and Leifweiden by her side, making notes on everything he saw.

Navas looked down and smiled sadly at her sister. Maybe Crooked Dancer would have new foods to try out here, as well.

She travelled on, past the nebulae, galaxies new and old, ghosts of the suns, the stars that shone so sweetly, and the nursery. She couldn't go back there, not with her sister… as much as she'd love to see the little baby stars. Finally, she could see a bright yellow star and knew that this was home.

As Navas got closer, she stopped. The entire solar system looked so different. She could even feel a wind. The planets looked far more spaced out than she remembered.

Planet Entanerus was surrounded by many small spheres, and it had a moon or planet that was as big as itself. Akin The Moon and Planet Navas, they looked so close and similar, it looked like a sibling planet for Entanerus. Planet Goston had little moons, as did Planet Crooked Dancer, which had a thin band of ice or glass surrounding its planet.

But it was Planet Polymir that looked the most radiant. The glass and ice from the creation of this new solar system, and the destruction of the glass bridges, bore a beautiful ring around it, a perfect embellishment to its quiet world.

Navas smiled and her eyes began to well with tears. Polymir had been so worried about meeting the Queen with his affliction, yet his planet was now the most wonderful sight in the solar system.

Getting closer, she saw that Planet Geadeous had a deep red scar etched into its surface, and looked far bluer, the heat of the clouds dampening. Navas looked at her own bleeding leg and wrists and thanked Geadeous. She had protected her family and the Queen, in their bleakest time.

Travelling past asteroids, Navas could see that Leifweiden's planet was now snow-free, bar the caps, and it was a rusty red. There were two little moons surrounding his planet, too, but they didn't look completely round.

The observatory had gone, and all that was left was the volcano. She wondered if it was warm on his planet, and wanted to visit as soon as she could.

Her own planet had lost most of its volcanoes. Its red, violent half was now green and blue throughout. Most of the planets were capped with the same green aura she'd seen on the iron ring, like little crowns of dancing light.

She hated seeing that the cratered Moon was now further from her home, and hugged Liras harder. Their connection, the ice tower, was also gone. She was glad Liras couldn't see this.
Planet Iros and Planet Celd Dion were unchanged. Although, without their keeper, the plants on Planet Celd Dion would not have survived.
Planet Iros looked more pockmarked and so small against the burning Sun. Navas could feel The Sun's heat, but she couldn't feel *their* energy anymore. Not the planets' electricity, storms or wind... not the rumble of volcanoes or rain. She couldn't feel their energy anymore, her family. She decided, there and then, that the planets would now only be named after their Heerajras. Iros and Leifweiden, her family. It was only who they were now.

Navas, without the bridge to walk across, crashed down on her own planet and cradled Liras. As soon as she felt the grass of her planet beneath her feet, she shook and then she cried hard, from the relief of being back home and the shock of losing her sister and her friends.

"My sweet girl…" She cried harder and buried her face in Liras's chest, and her shoulders shuddered as she cried. She carefully pulled the material away from her sister's face and examined her damage. Navas fell to her knees, and, out of her depths, a scream erupted from her. It was so loud, the clouds parted above her.

Navas, now releasing her tears, couldn't stop crying and, for the first time in their history, Glaruntia, in her golden glory, arrived on her planet, cape settling into the ocean and off the planet's edge. She stared at Liras's limp, pale body, and then at Navas, bloodied, her clothes torn, and crying so loudly she was incoherent. She heard snippets of 'they're all gone' and 'my sister is gone'.

She heard how The Quasar had terrified Navas and how she faced up to it. Glaruntia took a step back in surprise. Navas had faced The Quasar?

Glaruntia let Navas sob and then, taking her robe sleeve, knelt in front of her and wiped her tears, blood smattering on the silk.

Navas sniffed loudly. Glaruntia had never seen Navas's eyes so dull. They were now copper rather than a wonderful gold.

"Where are they? Where is my family?" asked Glaruntia.

Her bottom lip wobbled.

"He... ate them," replied Navas quietly. "Leifweiden... they're all gone."

Glaruntia closed her eyes tightly and Navas watched her hang her head. Glaruntia thought of Geadeous and battled the urge to cry herself.

"Alright, Navas."

"I should go and see their Kassels," said Navas lightly. "I should see if I can take some of their earth back." She leant to place Liras down, but Glaruntia held her sore wrist.

"Navas, no. You need to rest now. We both do."

Navas didn't understand, but Glaruntia refused to break eye contact.

"Your Majesty—"

She shook her head. "Call me Glaruntia. I am not to reign over just you." Her voice broke.

Navas smiled, her eyes shining from the tears. She stroked Liras's clay, cold cheek. "My sweet sister." She sighed deeply.

Glaruntia and Navas both ventured out to Liras's cratered dusty, dull moon. The deep, grey sand travelled slowly across the canyons. The palace was gone and there was no trace of the princess's abode.

Glaruntia, with one sweep of her hand, created a crevice where Liras could finally rest. Navas placed her sister down, almost reluctantly. Within seconds, Princess Liras became grey and crumbled into the same dark grey sand. Navas pressed her hand into the sand where her sister lay as Glaruntia watched on.

"I'll always care for you, my sister," whimpered Navas. "She's so far away... why couldn't she stay with me? My... moon and I have been tied forever."

"You will be, Navas," replied Glaruntia. "She'll be in your sky now, not on your planet."

Navas nodded absently. It wasn't the same. The knife wound in her heart would never heal.

Glaruntia held Navas's hand, and they both returned to Planet Navas.

They watched the white clouds roll across in the cornflower blue sky. Both sat, clasping their knees, side by side.

"I felt your energy out there," said Navas tonelessly. Glaruntia frowned. "I wonder how?" *Maybe it was the outburst*, she thought. "I'm glad. You're here now." Navas could barely believe she was, too. Thank goodness for Remanence.

A soft gust of wind brushed over them both and Navas relished it, her eyes closed. Glaruntia thought back, to when her daughter had her beautiful long, cloudlike hair and her eyes shone as bright as lanterns. She looked so hollow and defeated now.

"Thank you," Navas said to her Queen, her eyes still closed.

They both sat on the grass, in the warm sun, just to enjoy the easing winds. Tea was most needed, Navas realised, feeling slightly better at the mere thought of holding a hot mug of fragrant soaked ginkgo.

After a moment, Navas collapsed onto the grass from exhaustion.

When Navas came to, she went back to her room, her studio still as it was. Paintings were still to be signed off; the sink filled with bristly brushes.

Hers was the last Kassel to remain on the planets.

She lay in her bed and Glaruntia sat by her side, her cape weaving out of the entrance. As Navas tried to compete with falling asleep, vines and flowers began to grow all throughout her studio, engulfing her paintings and paintbrushes, suffocating the walls. Flowers sprouted from each corner, giving the impression that her home was born from a tree. Small lotus flowers began to grow from her wrists, painlessly. Navas was so tired, she didn't even acknowledge it.

"Sleep now, Navas. You can rest now," said Glaruntia quietly.

Navas dragged a green blanket over herself.

"Thank you, Your Majesty... oh, Glaruntia. I'm not tired, I'm sad. Let me rest for a while and then we can have tea together."

Glaruntia kissed Navas's forehead as she watched Navas struggle to keep her eyes open. She smiled as she pushed back strands of Navas's cropped hair away from her forehead.

"I am going to rest as well, daughter," she said softly. "My palace is gone. You were gone for so long. I wonder what you saw? I wonder who you met? I know you're feeling alone, but I can give you the gift of life. They will give you company and you will never be by yourself. I don't want you to ever be alone. You'll need to rest now."

Navas nodded sleepily and watched Glaruntia leave her room.

Hazily, Navas looked up past her half-roofed loft, as she had done so many times, and for once saw something different. She could see the planets, shining larger than the stars around them, as dusk fell, all in their new forms.

She raised her hand to reach out to them, and she saw the bright, red mark of Leifweiden. She smiled and moved her hand, as if cradling the red spot. As the sleepiness took over her, she turned to observe the horizon out of her window. In the sky, as The Sun was setting, she could see The Moon, shining as bright as a pearl, its glow lighting up the entire plain. Navas gasped as, despite the grey fields, The Moon could still shine as bright as before. She thought of the other planets, Entanerus and Goston, the lopsided Crooked Dancer, and Polymir with its new, wonderful set of rings. Geadeous with its mighty storms, the speedy Iros, and the dense, choking air of Celd Dion.

Her last thoughts were of Leifweiden, his kind smile and heart, and of her sister Liras. The last image she saw in her mind was Liras gazing up at a terracotta tree, its blushed leaves falling gently about her.

Navas smiled warmly at the memories they had shared, as she pulled the blanket over her head. Her Kassel and herself, body, hair and eyes, were covered in flowers and vines and fauna. Navas was now a part of her planet and would sleep forever, a being made of flowers, soon to be absorbed entirely by her planet.

***

A small lake bubbled near a field of tulips and Glaruntia placed her gold mitre in the waters. Soon, life would be born on this planet, and Navastratun wouldn't be alone.

She couldn't look at Navas's Kassel. It was completely taken over by flowers and plants now.

Glaruntia went back to her Sun and looked out across the solar system. She was glad that, when her own time came, her children wouldn't need to live in fear. Her buildings and city were all but gone now. Glaruntia wished she could land near the planets one last time but knowing that they were stark and alone made her reluctant to do so. She pulled a piece a paper from under her collar.

She took one last look at the sketch that Navas had drawn of her family and closed her eyes in happiness and pain. Her beautiful family could never be forgotten. Thanking Navas, she felt a great surge of anguish as she sank into the golden ocean of her star.

THE END

Printed in Dunstable, United Kingdom